Nobody's Savior

A collection of horror

Wesley Winters

SLASHIC HORROR
PRESS

Nobody's Savior

A collection of horror

Wesley Winters

Originally published in Australia by Slashic Horror Press in 2024.

SLASHIC HORROR
PRESS

ISBN-13: 978-0-9756380-1-9
Cover design by RoscoFly
Interior design by David-Jack Fletcher
Edited by David-Jack Fletcher

For those that are also suffering and struggling with their mental health. Even if you prefer healing through isolation the way I do, never hesitate to reach out if you need someone to talk to that understands.

Bigotry still exists, even when things seem safe on the surface. This hate is a lingering ghost that continues to haunt our community, whether it presents itself openly or nips at our heels in the dark. Keep you and yours safe.

Table of Contents

WHISPERS

When you look at the ground—really look at it—you'll see the movement.

I've been out here for two hours today, seated in a foldout chair at the edge of the lake. I've come with a book, which resides on my lap. As I give my eyes a rest from the text, I stare at the ground surrounding my feet. The dirt and grass appear still at first. But given a few seconds, it suddenly looks as if I'm surrounded by bugs crawling over my shoes and chair. I take in their movement and wonder how many of these creatures I crush with every step I take outside. It's both humbling and distressing.

It's not easy, but I blink and lift my eyes, returning them to the book I hold in my hands. The words shift, vibrate. The pages swirl into a vortex of ink, blackening their entirety. I toss the book away from my chair and rub my eyes with a fierceness that brings me pain. When I blink again, I lean forward and eye the ground once more. The bugs have swarmed over my library loan and swallowed it in seconds.

And then the movement speaks to me.

I hear whispers, hundreds of them overlapping one another, desperate to be heard above the other. The cacophony of voices is overwhelming and startling, sending me backward from my chair. I run. I don't look back. I don't return for my things. I report the book lost and pay a fee for its replacement. A small cost in the grand scheme of things.

Safety is priceless, but I am not safe. I am mistaken. The whispers follow me home.

I hear them again while putting my daughter to bed. They're distant but swelling by the minute. My little girl holds her pillow tight over her ears as she clenches her jaw in irritation. Does she hear them, too? I reach a hand to touch her shoulder and she startles. I ask her, "Is everything okay?"

She trembles and turns away. The pillow remains against her ears. I begin to feel a sickness spread across my chest. I exit the room in search of the invading whispers. My husband calls for me from the pantry, but I do not hear him. He's just another sound I swat away in an attempt to zero in on the source of my new hell. I'm outside a minute later, combing the yard barefoot and in my pajamas.

The ground is moving beneath me. Squirming. The voices are loud now, howling in my ears. They ring inside my head, painful and intoxicating. I feel drunk and stumble.

My husband is beside me now.

I don't know how much time has passed, how long I've been there in the grass, shivering and clawing at my skin. An ambulance is coming, he tells me. But he sounds so far away.

I regain consciousness in a white room, sterile and blinding. Why have the lights been left on? I want to plead for darkness, but I find myself immobilized. Not by machinery, but by invisible hands. They hold me against the bed and cover my mouth.

And they whisper.

You will forever question every step you've taken here.

GRIEF

The word *loss* meant nothing to me before Damion. I thought I understood it, even from an outsider's perspective, but then I fell in love with a man who died before we ever had a fair chance at a life together. We never went on vacation or made a home as one. I fell in love with a man that lived far enough from me that we could only see each other one weekend a month. And before we had spent even half a year together, he was taken away by the violent and stupid force of a drunk teenager on a joyride. Physically, Damion and

I only had twelve days together. But those twelve days were enough to wreck me.

We met at a horror convention for authors and their readers. While in line to see the same writer, we talked and felt an immediate spark. Seeing as we'd both driven several hours to attend the convention, we were staying overnight in nearby hotels. We ended up having dinner together and spent the night in Damion's room talking about books. It was a first date I'll never forget.

Losing Damion has left me feeling a strange mixture of hollowness and heaviness. I feel empty of love and meaning, but at the same time the world around me is weighing me down, pushing my face into the dark and telling me to eat it. Though my friends have been supportive in their own awkward ways, my family has told me to move on and get over it. "He was just a fling. You barely knew each other." But me and Damion spent every night on the phone talking. For six months, he was part of my routine. Not only that, he was the happiest part of my routine.

We took photos together every weekend we shared. However, in my grief, I've had trouble looking at them. They're in a shoebox under my bed, terrifyingly close at hand. When I lie my head down at night, I feel like Damion's eyes are burrowing into the back of my skull, begging for attention. I don't understand the guilt but it's there, and I feel traumatized by it.

The local news is warning us of a dangerous hurricane moving into the area tomorrow. I live near a stream running off from the river, so I'll no doubt experience some mild to heavy flooding. I've tried to prepare with sandbags along the walls but there's too much footage to cover. I do have a loft, so I'm considering moving my most valuable things up there until the storm passes. My furniture would be difficult to do alone, though, so I've managed to collect a few pallets to raise some of it up four or five inches. I've done this for my bed, the couch, and the sofa. I don't have enough pallets to do anything else. Now I just have to pray I don't flood inside too much—or at all.

There were times while raising my furniture I felt like it was pointless. Not because of the probability of my house flooding but because I don't care much about my stuff anymore. I don't care about anything anymore. Without Damion, the house seems to haunt me. I don't quite understand it—Damion never lived here with me—but the shadows have begun taunting me, reminding me of how alone I am. Anywhere there's a clear space, I've begun throwing papers and clothes about. The messier the space, the less alone I feel. I used to keep a very clean house, I'll tell you, but now I feel torn in two between cleaning and hiding the floors. And this is why I welcome the flood, on some level. I want my house torn apart and full of leaves and rock and sand. I want my carpets full of washed-out bugs and snakes. I want...disorder.

Maybe that's why, on some subconscious level, I left the shoebox on the floor beneath my bed.

I can hear the rain picking up outside. The winds will soon follow. From the couch, I stare at the images on the TV, not taking anything in. My Kindle is in hand but forgotten as I daydream. I imagine Damion is there beside me with a coffee. Though he is covered in bloody cuts, he appears fine. We have the windows ajar and are listening to the rain while we plan the day. He suggests moving the house around, giving it a fresh spin now that he's there, too. Right now, it's my space but it needs to become *our* space.

Without even realizing it, I've started rearranging things. I'm almost trance-like, unaware my daydream is bleeding into reality. Only, Damion isn't here. Not physically. Is he a ghost? I don't know if I believe in the afterlife, as much as it pains me to think he's just nothing and nowhere now.

I pushed the couch against the far wall, moved the sofa front and center with the coffee table, and placed the reading light beside it. The painting on the wall has been taken down and replaced by a photo of me and Damion outside the hotel the day after we met, right before we went our separate ways home. The magazines that had been splayed across the coffee table have also been changed. In their place is a small stack of books I've been meaning to read—books Damion bought and recommended to me—as well as a small succulent plant, a journal, and a pen. I'm not sure where I found some of these things because they were stowed away several months earlier. When the call came that Damion had been killed, I trashed my house and later hid anything that reminded me of him. Some of it gradually made its way back out of hiding, but these things did not.

A crack of thunder strikes and the house vibrates with a passing wave of force. It's gotten much darker outside, I realize, and the rain is torrential now. Winds are smacking against the house and pushing water from the stream onto the grass in foamy explosions. I take a step back from the window and move into the bedroom, all the while imagining Damion is there beside me. He says, "This looks like a bachelor pad," and swings his hands over the room in an exasperated gesture of disgust. "Where am I in it? Where is the love and partnership?"

I spend the next hour moving things in there while Damion points and prods me along. I clean up the mess from the floor and brace myself for the shadows of loneliness to stretch across the bare carpet. Instead, I turn and see Damion watching me with a comforting smile, his backside leaning against the dresser. Still, his injuries don't appear to register with him. Though his smile is thick with blood, it remains. So, I continue to clean. I throw away the trash that has accumulated on the nightstand and my desk, and I bring out the vacuum once all of my clothes have been moved to the hamper. As I vacuum, I block out all sound. I somehow forget all about the hurricane until the lights suddenly go dark and the vacuum becomes still.

"We've lost power," Damion says, pushing himself away from the dresser and moving to the window. I follow him and look outside. It's looking rough. Trees have fallen around the property and the yard is underwater. It's only a matter of time before the house begins to flood. Lightning overhead makes me flinch away from the window several feet, backing myself into Damion's arms. But his body is cold against mine, as if it isn't really there. Turning to confront him, I am alone in the bedroom.

The tears come and with as much force as the hurricane outside. I fall to the floor—the goddamned, clean floor—and tip onto my side with my arms wrapped around myself. I don't know how much time passes as I sob against the itchy fibers of the carpet. But the room is getting colder without the heat pump working. I want a blanket but cannot reach my bed from my place beside the dresser. With some difficulty, I force myself to stand and collect a woven throw to place over my shoulders and hug tight against my chest.

I leave the bedroom and glance toward the loft over the bookshelf and the mounted TV. There's a ladder mounted near the corner for me to use. Once I'm in the triangular shaped space, I inch toward the oval window and look out upon the driveway and road. The stream may as well have been running there all along—you can no longer see the pavement or dotted lines. There is also a large tree blocking passage a hundred yards beyond my mailbox, which is resting at an angle. It will be gone by the morning, if not sooner.

I turn away from the window and sort through the things I moved into the loft earlier for safe keeping. I find my medicine bag and retrieve my sleeping pills. Though I consider taking a handful, I settle on two and cuddle up to an ornamental pillow my grandmother made when I was a child. Despite the heavy winds and rain, I manage to fade into the darkness only minutes later, my head still aching from the tears I shed on my bedroom floor.

An enormous crash startles me awake some time later. I jolt up from the pillow and smack my head against the slanted ceiling, having temporarily forgotten I'm lying in the loft. I inch over to the edge and look below. The tree with my birdhouse and bird feeders has come down into the living room, tearing through the wall and window along the west side of the house.

Water is pouring into the house and rising before my very eyes. I'm lucky the tree—any tree, for that matter—didn't fall through the loft instead. Then again, maybe my death would have been for the best.

Exhausted, I manage to climb out of the loft, not wanting to face the damage before me. What was I even supposed to do about it? Get in the car and leave?

The house shakes with another thunderous roar from above. For a long minute, I just stand there in the water, looking at the exposed wall and the leaves piling up beneath the tree. This was what I'd wanted, wasn't it? *Disorder*. An excuse to give up, lie down, and let nature take its course. I don't know. Maybe it's been longer than a minute. I can't seem to move my legs in any direction. I don't feel the motivation to do anything about the storm or my destroyed house. How much longer will the hurricane last? Was I to seek refuge somewhere without being stupid enough to drive down the river of a road?

It seems like the room has flooded in no time at all. It's as high as my shins when I will myself to cross into the kitchen for a drink. For some reason, in that moment, all I can think about is having a shot of tequila. But instead of a shot, I tip the bottle back against my lips and gulp from it. Within seconds, I'm spewing the alcohol across the counter and coughing with tears in my eyes.

"Stop that!"

I turn and see Damion standing on the other side of the exposed wall, the rain drenching him. A horrendous gash along his forehead is being pushed down by the stream of water running down from his scalp and over his eyes. At his feet is the shoebox of our photos, floating on a stream out of the house and into the yard. I drop the tequila and give chase, screaming after it. My chest feels like it's crumbling under the force of a thousand blows as I lose sight of the shoebox. I slip outside as Damion vanishes behind a crack of lightning that strikes the lamp nearby. In the flash, I am blinded for a second, scared for my life. I'm surprised to feel anything of the sort but I don't have time to linger in the moment. I chase the shoebox down the driveway and toward the road. The water is high out here, up to my thighs. I struggle to push forward against the currents that seem to always oppose me.

"Wait!" I scream. "I'm not ready!"

The shoebox turns onto the road and floats further away from me. By the time I've reached the place my mailbox once stood, the shoebox of photos has gone too far for me to see through the storm. Defeated, I drop to my knees. The water crashes against my chest now, threatening to tip me under. I consider fighting it but instead bow my head as tears mix with the rain against my cheeks. A wave overcomes me a moment later, pressing me underwater and dragging me along the gravel of my driveway. I feel the sharp pricks across my face but I do not care. I shut my eyes and allow the flood to carry me back towards the house.

When I open my eyes, sunlight is breaking through the oval window behind me. I roll over and realize the storm has ended and that I am still in the loft. The shoebox had been a dream, more vivid than my own life in months.

I climb down the ladder in the corner and inspect the living room. There's no tree cutting through the wall, cleaving my house in two, but there is standing water. As I walk across the room, my slippers splash along the carpet. I look outside and see many downed branches and enormous puddles but the storm has passed. For reasons I can't define, I feel different. I turn away from the windows and enter the bedroom.

Why am I here? I wonder.

My legs compel me to move in a way they haven't in a long time. I approach the bed and take a knee beside it. As my sweatpants soak up water from the carpet, I crane my head to the side and look under the raised mattress. There's the shoebox of my memories with Damion, however few. I can see water staining all around its base, and ask myself what I should do. Instinctively, I reach for the box and pull it out. Sitting on the edge of the bed with the damp cardboard resting on my lap, I peel away the lid. Inside, the scattered stacks of photos

13

have curled from water damage. I take a handful out of the box and look through them. My chest is tight with panic but I push forward through the pictures, inspecting every last one of them.

"Are you ready?"

The voice comes from behind me, near the window. I twist to see Damion standing there, uninjured and wearing the very clothes he had the first time we met at the horror convention all those months ago. I reposition myself on the bed to face him, and lower the photos in my hands. Damion's eyes are drilling into me with worry. They're blue and as brilliant as they were in life. I feel something crack inside me but I don't fall apart. I close my eyes and take a deep breath. When I open them again, Damion is still there watching me. But his smile has returned.

"Are you ready?" he asks again.

"It won't be easy," I tell him.

"That's okay."

"What do I do now?"

Damion reaches out for the photographs in my hand. I pass them over and he looks through several of the memories with fondness. "Do you remember our plan?" he asks me.

"Which one?"

"The book."

I can't help but smile. I haven't thought of the book since Damion's death, not even when the journal appeared on the coffee table last night during my cleaning.

"You want me to write it without you?" I ask him, confused.

"You know the story," he says, turning the photographs so that I can see them. At the front, there's a young man I hardly recognize. He's happier than he's ever been, on the forest floor covered in mud and laughing. I remember the fall like yesterday. It's me in the picture, from when Damion took me hiking away from our campsite. The trip had been a mess but the kind you don't want to ever forget. Somehow I had, which hurt.

"Remember it now," Damion says, understanding my gaze on the photograph. "Remember all of it. And write our story. It doesn't have to be for them," he says, sweeping a hand toward the window behind him. "It can just be ours, if you want. But relive this for me, please."

I look down and see the journal on the bed beside me. I don't know how it got there, but I pick it up and feel its weight. It is no longer as heavy as it was when Damion first bought it for me. Back then, it felt intimidating. Now it feels light and electric in my hands.

"Then what?" I ask him, looking up once more.

Damion places the curled photographs onto the nightstand and smiles. "Fight. For the both of us. Fight for something as good as we had."

"I can't imagine finding something like that ever again."

"You will. I'll dissolve into you and always be there when you need me," he says, taking several steps towards me and leaning forward. "Just take this leap for me."

Our lips meet and I close my eyes. This time, I can feel his warmth as if he's really here. I disappear in that moment, not wanting to open my eyes and see the empty room I know awaits me. I wait until that warmth spreads to my chest and embraces the rest of me in a way only Damion could.

When I open my eyes, the lights throughout the house switch on. From the kitchen, the clock on the oven beeps, ready to be set. Elsewhere, the heat pump hums to life, as if the house is breathing once more.

I know I am.

GHOSTS OF HESSINGTON HILLS

Lendon Wells Community College had a tunnel connecting one parking lot to the other, exiting on the opposite side of the road, splitting the campus in two. Buildings A-C were on one side of Tetherman Road. Building D, the recreation center, and greenhouses were on the other. The tunnel was built long before the college but renovated when the school came along, and was almost the length of a school football field.

Inside the tunnel were lights that ran its length from the ceiling. They were cared for by the maintenance staff and monitored regularly, as were the emergency call boxes to campus security and the police. There was one stationed half way through the tunnel, and another outside each entrance. Though these emergency stations came with their own cameras, they showed nothing beyond a five foot radius. Nevertheless, the stations outside the entrances were capable of showing whoever entered or exited the tunnel during all hours of the day and night. It is for this reason no one has ever been able to explain the mass murder of 2008.

Tye Cameron, the new math teacher, knew nothing of the story when he accepted his teaching position and moved into town. He was from California, LWCC was located in Virginia. He and his husband, Chase, had crossed the country to start anew, following the loss of their bookstore and coffee shop. Covid had seen to that. Many small independent shops in their area fell during the pandemic. Though Chase had fought like hell to keep it above water—going as far as taking book and drink orders over the phone and delivering them all around town—it just wasn't enough to save them. They'd barely been scraping by as it was before the pandemic.

The locals contributed the tunnel killings to the ghost of Lendon Wells himself, the once-beloved mayor of Hessington Hills that died from suicide in the 1950s following his wife's murder. She had been on her way home from the library, cycling across Billingsby Bridge—which led into the main neighborhood over the creek—when a gang of young men robbed and raped her during the start of nightfall. Lendon Wells swallowed a shotgun days later, and left a note that read: *These lecherous men must be put down!*

Chase eyed his husband and chuckled. "And they believe that's enough to suggest his ghost slaughtered those seven students in the college tunnel?"

Tye met his husband's gaze and shrugged. "I guess so. They *were* all male, after all."

"So?"

"Apparently, there was a girl there, too, but she escaped untouched."

Chase scrunched up his face. "If that's true, then why doesn't anyone know what happened down there?"

Tye smiled, sheepish, and said, "Because the girl said it was Lendon Wells."

Chase gave a dramatic, non-believer laugh, and stood from their couch. "Um, *okay.*"

Following him into the kitchen, Tye checked their dinner on the stove. Chase did most of the work while Tye taste-tested and carried on conversation.

"So, what happened to the girl?" Chase asked while stirring a pot of seafood pasta sauce. A recipe he'd found on Instagram.

"She left Hessington Hills fifteen years ago, shortly after the murders. I don't know where she is now."

"Sounds like a load of horseshit."

"Probably, but it's still fun to work in some place that's considered haunted."

"I thought it was just the tunnel that was haunted."

"I think they consider the *town* haunted, but the tunnel is infamous for that particular slaughter."

Chase looked over his shoulder. "What else has happened here?"

"Unsolved murders here and there. I think the locals automatically tag them as Lendon Wells sightings."

His husband shook his head, amused. "Well, I guess it's a good thing we're surrounded by individuals with imagination. That should help us when I relaunch the shop."

Now that things were returning to normal—or, at least, the new normal—Chase had become dead set on bringing back Shelfside Magic. The plan was to save for a year before beginning the process all over again. In the meantime, Chase had taken a waitering position at a seafood restaurant in the next town over. Though he was making good tips there, he was hoping to get in the kitchen instead. He had a plan to bring his boss a buffet of food but had to first learn seafood cuisine—he was still new to preparing it. Shelfside Magic had served exquisite sandwiches and snacks, never seafood.

"Some of the other teachers invited us to a party this Saturday," Tye said as he collected a beer from the fridge. "Will you be available?"

"As long as I can leave for work by three. When is the party?"

"It's a cookout. They said eleven or so."

"Then it should be fine. Do they know you're married?"

Tye held up his hand to wiggle his ring finger. "Of course."

"Do they know you're married to a *guy*?"

"Yes. No one cares. Not here. We're not far enough south for it to be a problem."

"Being in a college town probably helps." Chase shrugged.

"Probably."

"Well...what's the plan for tonight?"

Tye moved up behind his husband and wrapped his hands around Chase's waist. "A movie with dinner?"

"What did you have in mind?"

"Hmm... *Midnight Mass*?"

"That's a show."

"Whatever. I've had it on my Netflix list for too long."

"What's it about?"

"Something with a crazy reverend, I think. I don't really know, but it's Mike Flannagan."

"Who?"

"He's the creator and director. He's done a lot of great horror."

21

Chase moved his pot off the burner and turned to face Tye. "Sure, I guess. Why not? Let's get spooky tonight. But don't you need to prepare for tomorrow's classes?"

"Already done. I got a lot set up in advance for the first month."

"Nothing to grade?"

"I took care of it before coming home."

"Look at you, *overachiever*," Chase teased, kissing Tye on the side of the neck.

"Now, now. We haven't even had dinner yet." Tye shied away from his husband. "Allow *Midnight Mass* to get us in the mood."

Chase snorted as he turned to plate their food. "Like that's going to get me going."

Tye squeezed his husband's ass and left to get the table set up. "Horror makes me feel alive. The mood follows."

"Mr. Cameron?"

Tye looked up from his desk at the student raising their hand. "Yes?"

"Where are you from?" the girl asked. Her name was Piper and she'd proven to be a talkative student.

Tye smiled at her. "What does that have to do with your worksheet?"

"I'm done."

Several other students raised their heads to pay attention.

"I'm from California," Tye told her.

"What part?"

"Humboldt."

A male student joined in. "Oh, shit, Mr. C. You got any weed on you?"

Several others laughed.

"How about you all get back to your worksheets?" Tye said.

"What brought you to Hessington Hills?" Piper asked instead.

"A fresh start," he told her.

"Did something happen back home?"

"We lost our business during the height of Covid."

"What kind of business?"

"A book shop."

"What kind of books do you like to read?"

"Horror. Suspense. Thriller. Mystery."

"You should try taking one of your books down into the tunnel then," Piper suggested with a mischievous grin. "It can be quite an experience at night."

"Is that so?" Tye said, humoring her. "Have you tried it?"

"I have. It's safe for girls to do."

"But not guys?"

"You'll be tempting fate," she told him. "And going in a group obviously doesn't protect you."

Tye smiled but didn't know what else to say. He returned his eyes to the work he was grading and let the classroom fall back into a comfortable silence. It didn't last very long, as more and more students finished their sheets and began talking amongst themselves. Tye asked how many were still working and found most were done.

"Alright, so was there anything there you weren't familiar with?" he asked, standing from his desk and moving in front of his smartboard. "A lot of those problems are based on the curriculum for the first semester. The less we have to cover in detail, the faster we can get through things."

A quiet student raised their hand from the back.

"Yes?"

"Are we going to be forced to solve equations in specific ways? They're always changing."

Tye brought up a document on the board that showed the Graphical Method for solving a linear equation. "Though we will go over the ways the state wants things taught, I don't personally care how you solve the problem, as long as you solve it without using a calculator."

Another hand shot up. "You don't want us using a calculator for...anything?"

"Only when necessary. You should be able to do most of the math by hand."

Heads turned around the classroom. A lot of his students didn't appear very confident.

"You know how to do multiplication and division, correct?" Tye asked them. He'd heard of schools doing away with such things. Instead, students were using their tech to answer everything for them.

"I know my basic tables," the same student replied. "Like 8 by 6."

"What if I asked you to multiply 41 by 37?"

The student opened their mouth, then closed it.

Tye tried not to sigh too loud. *Shit*, he thought, checking the time. They had twenty minutes left.

"Okay, new plan. We will catch you all up on the basics first."

Once he was finished with his last class for the day, Tye considered going home to do his planning. But Chase was gone for the night and wouldn't be back until after eleven. It was only three in the afternoon, so he decided to hang back in his room to work instead. It was easier there with his smartboard and paperwork all in reach. Taking tests home to grade was fine, but he felt planning was always easier to do at the source.

He'd decided to redesign his week of lectures to better prepare his classes with the basics they should have been taught long ago, in hope that the rest would come with better understanding as a result. Before he knew it, hours had passed and he was getting hungry. He'd already eaten the lunch he'd brought with him, so he'd need to leave to find something else. He finished up what he was doing, gathered his satchel, and left the classroom.

Outside, he headed toward the covered stairs leading down into the tunnel. His car was parked on the other side of Tetherman because it was the side of the road he arrived from every morning and easier to reach during traffic. Despite its supposed hauntings, the tunnel had yet to bother him. It was well lit and clean. To his knowledge, no one had died there since the incident fifteen years earlier, and there was a part of him that was convinced the story he'd been told was well-exaggerated for the purpose of entertainment.

As he passed beneath Tetherman Road, so did many others. He was almost on the other side when Piper appeared ahead of him and called for his attention.

"Mr. Cameron!"

Tye looked up from his walking daze and spotted Piper alongside two of her girlfriends. "Hello, Piper," he said, hoping to pass them without being sucked into conversation. His stomach was growling uncomfortably now.

"Do you think you'll try it?" she asked as they neared.

"Try what?"

"Reading down here some night."

"Oh. I don't think so. Where would I sit?"

Piper paused to engage with him. Reluctant, Tye did the same, but with his body only half turned to show he had no intention of stopping for long.

"There are benches all throughout the tunnel, Mr. Cameron," she said. "Don't make excuses!"

He laughed at her ribbing. "I don't see the point in reading down here."

"For the challenge," she said, narrowing her eyes and smiling. "It's a rite of passage if you're new to the area. All the guys do it sooner or later."

"Read in the tunnel?"

"Well, not *read*, necessarily, but come down here during the night."

"If it happens organically, it happens," he said, taking a step forward, looking to leave. "Until then, I need to find some food."

"Have you tried Orange Michaels?"

"What a peculiar name."

"You'll get it once you're there."

Tye shrugged with a smile. "Okay."

Another step toward the exit.

"It's on the corner of Wilcox and Vibe. They make awesome sandwiches and have a baked goods section, too."

"Okay, I could go for a sandwich. Thanks for the recommendation."

At last, they were parting ways. A minute later, Tye was climbing the stairs back outside. He found his car and got inside. The heat was brutal, sinking into his skin and drawing out sweat from places he didn't want to think about. As he cranked the A/C and rolled up his sleeves, he considered the restaurant Piper had suggested and decided he'd go ahead and look it up on Maps. The eatery was only a minute down Tetherman in the short downtown stretch of Hessington Hills leading to the pier. He then checked his messages. He had one from Chase saying he'd asked his co-workers about Lendon Wells and was told several stories he wanted to share with Tye later.

After sending a quick reply, Tye pulled out of the parking lot and turned onto Tetherman Road. He was starving.

The name now made perfect sense.

On the wall opposite the counter was an enormous photograph of two shirtless men with vibrant tans standing side by side on the beach with footlong subs in their hands and big smiles on their faces. The owners were both named Michael and were, quite literally, orange from their time in the sun (or under a lamp). Beneath the photograph was a slogan of sorts that read: 'UNLIKE SOME PEOPLE, WE MAKE THIS LOOK GOOD'.

Tye chuckled when he first saw it. Though the men were far too tan for his liking, they were attractive nonetheless. Both had chiseled chests and abs from regular workouts—there was no way they could be in that shape without hitting the gym on a daily basis—and strong chins. In fact, they looked alike.

I guess there's some credence to partners mirroring one another, he thought, tempted to ask if they were actually siblings their parents named the same as a cruel joke. But neither owner was present behind the counter. Instead, there was a teenager, maybe nineteen, with long hair and glasses waiting for Tye to place his order.

"You're the new teacher, aren't you?" the kid asked when Tye approached.

Gotta love small towns, he thought.

"Yeah, I am."

"Have you been in the tunnel yet?"

Tye resisted the urge to roll his eyes. "Yeah, every day."

"At night?"

Tye tried to study the menu above the kid as he answered. "No, not at night."

"You should try it. The tunnel gets spooky as shit."

Tye smiled to humor the kid and placed his order. While he waited for it to be made, he pulled out his phone

29

to check bookstagram for new reading recommendations. He was reading a synopsis and early review for the next Hailey Piper novel when the boy announced his order was ready.

As Tye collected the bag he was being handed, the boy said, "Whenever you do decide to try your rite of passage, make sure to post about it online first."

"Why?"

"That way people know where to look if you go missing."

Tye raised an eyebrow to the boy and downturned a lip, trying to decide if he was being teased or threatened. The boy looked almost clueless with his goofy smile and long hair. After a few moments, Tye said, "Okay," and left the shop.

He would be eating at home instead, he decided.

A little after nine, he had finished his work and retired to the couch to watch more of *Midnight Mass*. Chase wasn't interested in continuing it but Tye had expected as much; Chase didn't care for anything dark in tone. Tye, on the other hand, found horror and its relatives to be his bread and butter.

At some point, he fell asleep without meaning to. It was the slamming of the front door after 11 that made him startle awake and look over the backside of the couch. Chase appeared around the corner a moment later, pacing back and forth, annoyed about something.

"What's going on?" Tye asked, standing and pausing the show.

Chase grunted and grabbed a beer from the fridge. "Things were good most of the night, but—"

"But what?"

"A couple guys tried jumping me in the parking lot as I was leaving. They probably thought the gay guy wouldn't know how to fight or something, but I stood up to them and they scared off pretty easily."

"You're okay then?" Tye asked, hugging his husband.

"Yeah, just pissed. I was hoping there wouldn't be any homophobic assholes here."

"What makes you think this was targeted like that?"

"They knew enough about me to call me faggot."

"So, you think they specifically wanted to bother *you* because you're gay?"

"That's how it seemed."

"How old were they?"

"Maybe college age."

Tye pursed his lips. "I think they're the minority, babe. I don't think many people here are like that. Not from what I've seen, and I'm at the college constantly. Plus, that word is a pretty common slur."

"I hope you're right."

Tye rubbed his back. "Have you eaten tonight?"

Chase shook his head. "Not really. But I'm not hungry. Just mad. Can we just go to bed and cuddle for a bit with *Gilmore Girls* on?"

"Yeah, sure. I was actually snoring on the couch when you walked in. I should be able to fall back asleep pretty quickly."

They turned off everything in the living room before leaving for the other side of the house. While Chase changed out of his work clothes, Tye brushed his teeth. They were just about to settle into bed when they heard something smash outside.

"What the hell was that?" Tye said.

Chase hurried out of the bedroom and down the hall to the front door, grabbing the baseball bat sticking out of their umbrella stand. Tye followed, but from several feet back. Outside, they saw several figures disappearing into the darkness of the street. In their driveway, Chase's car had a broken window. Glass littered the driveway beneath the driver side door.

"Motherfuckers!" Chase yelled, leaning inside his car for a closer look and dropping the baseball bat. "They threw a fucking cinderblock through my window." He reached in, unlocked the door, and yanked it open. He removed the cinderblock and tossed it into the yard. He then leaned back inside his car and continued cursing.

"What is it?" Tye asked, scanning their surroundings.

"I think the fucking thing broke my gear shaft. Can you bring me my car keys?"

"Sure." Tye tore his eyes from the dark road and returned inside. He found his husband's keys on the table by the door and hurried them back outside to Chase.

"Come on, come on…" Chase turned over the engine and tried shifting the car in reverse, but the shaft was bent awkwardly out of place and wouldn't move properly. "Fuck!"

Tye continued to scan the road and yard. "Will that be expensive to fix?" he asked.

"Probably, but I don't know," Chase grumbled, climbing out of the car after shutting it off. "Let's call the cops and file a report. Hopefully, those assholes don't come back."

"Do you think it was the guys from work?"

"If it was, they followed me for miles or already knew where I lived. Either way, that's…not good."

"Make sure to tell the police about that parking lot incident then, just in case."

"Help me patch this window real quick, and then we will get the cops here."

As Tye followed his husband inside, he collected the baseball bat from the ground and took one last look into the darkness. Were they being watched? He felt like there were eyes upon him and he didn't like it.

Not one fucking bit.

When it came time to get up for work the next morning, Tye was dead exhausted from being up so late. Though the thugs never came back to torment them further, he couldn't stop jumping at every sound he heard and every shadow passing by their window. Even Chase was on edge for the night. Lucky for him, he didn't need to be up early like Tye. However, without a working car, he'd have to Uber to work.

Classes were torturous. More than once, Tye almost fell asleep while waiting for his students to finish their assignments. He even withdrew from the time he'd normally spend lecturing in favor of worksheets that provided examples prior to the unsolved problems.

The following day was the barbeque with his fellow teachers, but Tye wasn't so sure now about going. He wondered if the group from last night were students of his or not. And if so, did any of these teachers acting friendly know his husband had been targeted? Would Tye be next? He half-expected his car to be vandalized when he left from work that day. Even the walk through the underground tunnel left him uneasy, though not for the reason of Lendon Wells. He couldn't help but think of Chase getting jumped in the parking lot. What if that happened to him? Tye wasn't the fighting type. His husband was the muscle in their relationship. He was more of the timid, friendly guy that people liked, and as such he rarely suffered at the hands of bullies growing up. He was lucky in that sense—he seemed to bring out the best in people, rather than their ugly sides.

When he returned home midafternoon, Tye tried their front door without his keys to make sure it hadn't been unlocked by someone. When it refused to budge, he sighed in relief. Once inside, he checked the back door and all the windows to make sure everything was locked as it should be. Then he spread out his papers on the dining room table and got to work on his grading. Chase was expected home around seven, in time for dinner. Tye was looking forward to it.

Despite his anxiety and exhaustion, the day had been smooth enough. Nobody asked him to stay in the tunnel at night this time, which he appreciated. Everyone had done their work without pissing him off with incessant talking or playing on their phones. His lunch, which had come from the cafeteria, was small but surprisingly good. So why did he feel like shit? Had his husband really got in his head so bad? Did they have bigots here in town to worry about?

When Chase returned home, he brought a pizza and breadsticks inside with him. Tye practically jumped up from the table in joy at the sight of food—he had been growing hungry by the minute since getting home. As he rushed his husband to grab a slice while kissing him on the cheek, he asked, "Any problems at work today?"

Chase shook his head and said, "No. But my manager checked the security footage from last night for me."

"And?"

"The file was deleted."

Tye looked at Chase and saw that his husband looked grave. "Wha-what does that mean?"

"It means someone working at my restaurant was in on it. Or at least knew one of the guys. So, they decided to hide the evidence."

"Oh, for fuck's sake…"

"Right." Chase sighed and pressed his lips in a tight line. "I have a feeling I'll have to set some people straight before long."

"How so?"

"By beating the ever-living-shit out of them the next time they try something. I need to send a message: don't fuck with us."

Tye had a love-hate relationship with this side of Chase. On one hand, he felt safe with Chase. Protected. Avenged, if need be. But he also worried about Chase going too far and ending up in jail or worse, dead. His husband had a dark side to him despite his lack of interest in dark entertainment. He was definitely not someone you wanted to cross.

"Let's just eat, sweetie," Tye said. "We can watch a movie tonight or play a game of Scrabble or something. And tomorrow we have the cookout, which should be fun."

"You still want to go to that?"

"I think so."

"You're not looking at your teachers differently?"

"I've been anxious all day, questioning the motives of everyone around me. I hate that feeling. I'd like to believe no one was actually targeted and that last night was a fluke that won't happen again."

"Fine. We can go. Maybe we'll learn something while we're there."

"Like what?"

"Maybe something related to last night."

Tye opened his mouth to argue but decided to let the conversation die. Instead, he shoved his pizza into his mouth and turned on the TV.

Sex that night was frenzied thanks to Chase's pent-up aggression. Though it went on longer than usual, they started early enough that they were sleeping by ten. Though Chase wasn't as tired as Tye, his mind was too preoccupied to focus on anything like a movie or a game. He was sleeping soon after sex. Tye took longer to pass out, but when he did it was a deep sleep. Neither of them woke when their front door was tagged by someone with spray paint. It wasn't until they were on their way to the barbeque the next day that they saw the poorly applied message.

GO BACK TO CALI, QUEERS

Chase clenched his fists. "We're installing security cameras this weekend. And buying a gun."

Before Tye could reply, his husband stormed away from the door and to the car. Tye looked at the message once more and cursed. Was this the work of a small group of people, or did the bigotry run deeper in the town than they realized?

The drive over to the barbeque was quiet and awkward. Tye worried Chase might make a scene around everyone at some point, and considered turning the car around. Neither of them wanted to go in the first place. Tye was just trying to integrate himself into their new community and make connections, and attending the barbeque was a quicker way to do that. Otherwise, he would have to talk to random teachers on campus, or approach strangers out in public. Neither option sounded all that appealing, even for someone as likable as Tye.

"Should we just turn back?" he asked Chase.

"I don't want to keep you from going," his husband replied.

"I know, but I'm a little worried now."

"About what?"

"About you. And I think the mood is pretty much dead now. I'm not really feeling up to small talk with people I hardly know."

"Are you sure?"

"I guess."

Chase watched him drive for a moment before facing forward. "What if we just drop you off and I go drive around until you're ready to be picked up? That way you don't have my sour puss bringing you down."

Tye didn't want to be left alone, but it was true his mood would improve if his angry husband wasn't there to keep him on edge.

"Promise to keep your phone on you?" he asked. "If things are going poorly, I want to know I can quickly get you back for me."

"Of course. I'll make sure not to go far, that way I can rescue you in a flash."

Tye sighed and agreed to the plan.

They pulled up to the curb of the sidewalk several minutes later. There were cars filling the driveway and lining the road. As Tye climbed out of the car and Chase moved around to the driver's seat to take over, he studied the house and listened to the muted chatter flowing out of the backyard.

"I feel weird," he admitted to Chase.

"In what way?"

"I'm not sure. You know I can be a social butterfly and make friends easily, but..."

"What?"

"It hasn't felt natural here yet. It's like I've retreated into my shell for some reason. I can't explain it."

"I'm sure the last couple days haven't helped," Chase said, taking Tye by the sides of his arms and facing him. "Look, sweetie. We're someplace new, starting over. This is stressful. This is, at times, a minefield being navigated. But between the two of us, you're the strong one. You know, socially."

They both laughed.

"So, if a barbecue is too much for you, then we won't make it." Chase joked. "But seriously, you can handle this. You're not quick to anger and suspicion the way I am. You'll feel better once you're back there and without me to taint your mood. I'm sure of it. And if something *does* come up, just call me back."

Tye nodded. "Okay."

They kissed goodbye and parted ways. As Tye headed up the driveway of cars, Chase drove away behind him.

Here goes nothing, Tye told himself, taking several deep breaths.

He walked a line of stepping stones between the house and garage and stepped through a picket gate into the backyard. There were at least twenty guests scattered about, talking and drinking. On the porch, he spotted their host,

Bill Madder, at the grill with his wife. He had spoken to Bill in the hall several times since his invite. Each conversation had been brief, but the man's happiness seemed genuine, as did his relentless enthusiasm, like that health nut in *Parks and Recreation*.

Everyone else was either a complete stranger or someone he'd waved to or greeted in the hallway. He recognized some of the faces, sure, but he hadn't talked to them yet. Couldn't tell you their names or what they taught. Others were spouses and partners that he'd never seen before. Without Chase, he felt naked in this crowd of couples.

"Tye! Come over here a sec," Bill called to him from the porch with a wave.

Tye turned and headed up the steps toward Bill.

"Where's your husband?" Bill asked.

"He's had a bad morning," Tye told him. "Well, a bad week, actually. But this morning was a continuation of it and he was not in a very social mood, as a result. Not that I could blame him. I almost didn't come either because of it."

"Well, shoot. What happened? If you don't mind me asking."

"We seem to have been targeted by some bigots in the area," Tye said with a sigh. "He was jumped at work. Then later that night, someone broke his car window and gear shaft with a cinderblock. And this morning we woke up to a message painted on our front door."

Bill looked at him with genuine shock on his face. Tye didn't believe it to be fake, which gave him a burst of relief.

"You're kidding me," Bill said with disgust. "Around here that's happening?"

"It looks that way, though I'm trying to brush it all off as coincidence."

"This all happened in a matter of a couple days?"

Tye nodded.

"I think I'd have to agree with your husband. As horrible as it sounds, I think you may have a group—a *small* group, hopefully—that has chosen to wage war with you. As far along as this area has come over the years, we are a college town, and as such outsiders are frequently present. This could even be a group of assholes visiting family or friends in town. Maybe they don't even live here and will be gone by next week."

"I hope it's just that."

"Me too, bud. Get yourself a beer from the fridge or this cooler by my feet. And what do you want to eat? I've got this pad of paper right here for order taking."

The barbeque got easier for Tye from there. Most people were friendly, though he tended to hang around Bill and his wife as much as possible since he was comfortable with them. More than once, Chase texted him to make sure things were going alright, to which Tye told him they were. A little after 1 p.m., conversation and food turned to games in the yard. There was horseshoes, croquette, poker, and cornhole. Tye really loosened up at this point, hopping from team to team through each game present. No one struck him as a bigot along the way. He didn't get the impression people were putting on acts around him. By the time 3 p.m. was nearing, Tye felt confident in telling Chase this group of teachers had nothing to do with the attacks on them.

I've got to get to work, Chase texted him. *Can I keep the car then? You have a teacher drive you home or you order an Uber?*

Tye told him that would be fine and returned to his game of horseshoes. He was terrible at it, but most people were a little drunk at this point and throwing them at random, so it didn't matter. Another hour passed before people began saying their goodbyes and leaving. Though Tye had been friendly with numerous couples by this point, he decided to call an Uber rather than ask for a ride from anyone.

He was dropped off out front of his house a little after four. The driver made a comment about the message spray painted across his door—"What asshole did that?"—before leaving Tye to head inside. The fact the driver had said anything along those lines helped Tye further relax about their situation. People in this town weren't bad, there was just a bad element somewhere in the mix. He wondered if they were

43

even residents or just visiting, as Bill suggested. He hoped they were only around temporarily, that way he and Chase wouldn't have to start a manhunt with the police in tracking down the people responsible.

Before heading inside the house, Tye went into the garage to see if they had any paint that matched the front door. There was some white in the corner mass of supplies, but it wasn't the same shade.

Doesn't matter, he told himself. *I'll just repaint the entire door with this then.*

Though he took the can out of the garage, he ended up leaving it by the front door for later. For one, he wasn't sure if it was enough paint (this wasn't the sort of thing he had much experience in doing), and two, he was a bit drunk. He could wait until tomorrow to fix up the door with Chase, before or after they shopped for security equipment.

Inside, he dropped himself onto the bed with a relieved, happy sigh, and passed out. Hours passed in an instant, and he woke to Chase shaking his shoulder, saying, "Babe. Babe, get up."

Tye rolled over and sat up, his head heavy still. "What? What is it? What's the time?"

Chase looked at his watch and said, "A little after one in the morning."

"Jesus, really?"

"Yeah. When did you come to bed?"

"Uh… After the cookout."

"Wow, you've been asleep that long already?"

"Passed out. We were drinking and playing games."

"Well, at least you had fun."

Tye rubbed his eyes and headed to the bathroom to splash water onto his face. "How did work go?" he asked along the way.

"Pretty uneventful. Nobody wants to talk about the missing security footage. They're being dodgy because they know shit. I think I'm going to have to quit and find a new job."

Tye smacked his face with water several times before toweling off. As he returned to the bedroom, he said, "I get it. And you have my blessing to look for something else. Maybe you can just stay at home for a bit and do some remote work. I know most of it seems to pay like shit, but it's just temporary."

"I guess. And it's not like I have a car at the moment until we get mine fixed. So working from home makes sense."

"Exactly."

Chase waited a beat before asking, "So nothing fishy at the party?"

"Not at all. Everyone was super friendly. Nobody acted suspicious or anything. I really don't think any of my co-workers have anything to do with this targeting."

"Damn. I was hoping for a lead."

Tye bit the inside of his cheek. "Bill suggested our problem might go away on its own. He thinks it could be some friends or family visiting a college student."

"That would be good," Chase admitted. "I hope he's right."

"Me too."

"Did you get that can of paint out of the garage?"

"Yeah, for the door tomorrow."

"Sunday is going to be busy for us, I guess."

"Yeah, but that's okay. It'll be the most time we've spent doing stuff together in a couple weeks."

"That's true." Chase nuzzled up to his husband and they kissed. "You still drunk?"

"No. Just…heavy-headed."

"You can't handle much movement then, can you?"

"Better to keep it very simple."

"I'll do my best," Chase said with a chuckle, kissing the side of Tye's neck and placing both hands around his waist.

Sunday morning, there was nothing new to discover. Tye took that to be a good sign the assholes had moved on with their lives. Chase wasn't so quick to jump to that conclusion, but he was relieved nonetheless.

46

After breakfast, they spent the morning shopping for security equipment and supplies to paint the door. While talking with a technician at the store about the cameras, Chase asked the man where he could buy a gun and how the process worked. Tye wandered around at this point, uneasy with the conversation.

When they returned home, they got to work and stayed busy until dinner. It rained a little as they ate, making them relieved they had done the door that morning. After dinner, Tye laid out his school papers across the dining table and began going over everything for the week. Chase dragged himself away to take a bath. Both men were tired and more than ready for bed. By the time Tye was finished, the rain had stopped and neither of them felt like doing anything else. So, they went to sleep.

Tye didn't know what time it was when he woke, but he turned toward the window in his groggy state and saw the face of a barn owl against the pane. He didn't think much of it at the time, but in the morning he began to question whether or not he'd dreamed it.

Because the problem was there were no tree limbs anywhere close to that window on the second floor. So either the owl had awkwardly perched on the window frame or...

Or what? Somehow hovered in front of the glass while staring in at Tye and his husband?

It must have been a dream. Tye even went outside after his shower to shine a flashlight up at the window and look for a way an owl could spy on them. But there was nothing to grip as far as he could see. Nothing that extended far enough for the glass to make it possible for an owl to rest its feet.

But as Tye turned back to the house to get ready, he noticed two indents in the grass, about thirty or so inches apart. He took a knee beside them and saw that they were both rectangular, vertically facing the house.

"No…"

He hurried inside to wake Chase. "What? What is it?" his husband asked, groggy.

"I hope I'm just imagining things, but—"

"What?"

"I think someone had a ladder against the house last night to spy on us."

This got Chase sitting up. "What?"

Tye led him outside to the marks and showed his flashlight on them while explaining his late night sighting of a barn owl at their window. Chase examined the indents in the grass and cursed. The ground was still soggy from the rain Sunday evening, making the punctures easier to see than they would have been otherwise.

As Chase stood to look up at their bedroom window, he said, "You thought you saw an owl?"

"After I found these marks, it occurred to me the face must have been a mask."

"Jesus, that's creepy as shit."

"Yeah."

Chase looked toward the road. If someone had placed a ladder against the house, even for just a minute, wouldn't someone else have noticed? Granted, they hadn't even woken up for it, so maybe the people were quiet enough to not raise any alarms.

"The cameras!" Chase yelled, snapping his fingers. "Do they face this direction at all?"

"You set them up, not me."

Chase rounded the house and looked around. They had a camera over the front door, another atop the garage exterior, and two in the backyard at each corner. There weren't any in the front except for above the door. "I wonder what the range of that is," he said to Tye, mostly thinking out loud. "At the least, it should show someone crossing our yard with a ladder, don't you think?"

"I would assume so." Tye shrugged.

Chase headed inside fast, Tye on his heels. "Let me get my phone and check the feed."

"While you do that, I'm going to get my things together for work," Tye replied. He was behind schedule that morning and was sure to be late for his first class if he didn't get himself together soon.

While collecting his papers into his briefcase and brewing a cup of coffee, he heard Chase curse from upstairs. A moment later, his husband was bounding down the stairs with his phone to show Tye a recording. "Look at this shit," he growled, handing over the phone.

Tye watched as two figures wearing owl masks carried a wooden ladder across their front lawn and disappeared off the side of the screen.

"Shit."

"That's right," Chase said, snatching the phone back. "You did see a fucking owl last night, but it was a creeper. What the fuck do these assholes want with us?"

Tye didn't reply. He knew the question wasn't meant to be answered by him. Chase already had his thoughts on the matter. These people were tormenting them because they didn't like gays. It was pure and simple. The question now was how to catch them in the act and have them arrested for their hate crimes.

"What now?" Tye asked as they returned upstairs for him to get dressed. He'd been wearing a robe since leaving the shower twenty minutes earlier.

Chase gnawed on his bottom lip as he paced around their bedroom. "I'm getting a gun today," he said after a minute. "Then I'm going to stay up the next night or two or however many it takes to catch these guys red-handed."

"And do *what* with the gun?" Tye's question was laced with fear.

"Whatever I have to," Chase said, meeting his worried gaze. "In Virginia, there's no waiting period. I can be home with a firearm this afternoon."

Tye took a deep breath and walked away. He needed to get going to work.

Classes seemed to drag for Tye because he was anxious. When Bill found him during his lunch period to invite him out for drinks, Tye was relieved to be offered a distraction. He wasn't the type to go to bars, especially without Chase, but the barbeque had reminded him he needed to let loose from time to time to keep his head on straight. Tentative, he accepted the invite and told Bill he'd make sure with his husband it was okay.

"Bring him along," Bill said, his usual happy self. "I need to meet the man behind the legend!"

"I'll ask him if he will," Tye said. "But don't take it personally if he turns us down. He hates bars, and you can't really blame him considering, uh..."

"Did something happen?"

"Yeah, unfortunately. A few years ago when we were first dating, we were confronted at a bar on vacation. It didn't go well."

Bill shook his head sadly and said, "That's horrible. But with me and the gang, you won't have to worry. I assure you, we have your back."

"Thanks, Bill. I'll confirm with you later about everything."

Once Bill had returned to his own classroom, Tye sent a text to Chase about the invite. He wasn't at all surprised when Tye replied minutes later with, *No fucking way. But you have fun. Let me know if there's any trouble.*

It was the first time they'd talked since that morning. Tye was tempted to ask how his husband's morning had gone and if he'd bought a gun or not, but he knew his anxiety would only get worse if he thought about such things. It seemed best to avoid the topic altogether and just focus on school for the time being.

And though he tried to do just that, Tye couldn't help but imagine his husband at a shooting range. Though the image of Chase firing a gun and keeping them safe turned him on, he also abhorred firearms—they fucking scared him. So, his mind continued to wander back to them as the day crawled on.

Hours later, while Tye was preparing his lessons for the next day, Bill swung by to see if he would be going to the bar or not.

"Yeah, I'm coming," Tye said. "But Chase won't be joining us as I suspected. When are you going?"

"I think we're heading over now. I can drive you if you want. The bar is only a walking distance from here, you know. Right down the street at the corner. The college kids love that."

Tye chuckled. "I bet they do."

"That's why there are constantly cars in our parking lot here. People leave them behind to go drinking."

"Do they stumble back for them after?"

"Not until the morning. *Usually*," he added. "I'm not going to say DUIs don't happen around town, because they do. But not as often as you might expect with a bar so close to campus."

Tye stood from his desk and collected his things. "Well, I guess I'll tag along with you and just walk back later."

"Let's just drop your stuff off at the car along the way," Bill told him. "No need to carry a briefcase with us all night."

He was still terrible at darts, he learned. And it wasn't because of his drinking—he'd had very little. Only two beers to loosen up. The same went for everyone in the group. No one was getting drunk like they had at the barbeque. This was just an evening to blow off steam after a long day of work. Tye was glad to have joined Bill and the others, though he didn't want this to become a new habit. Chase would feel left out, he knew.

He ate dinner there at the bar, which was surprisingly good. It was no wonder so many teachers and students came by The Wells Tavern after classes. There was a variety of drinks, good food (mostly appetizers), darts, pool tables, and a clean setting. This wasn't a dive bar by any means—it was well-kept and well-managed. Though Chase avoided such places ever since their incident in 2017, Tye thought maybe he could talk him into trying this place out some evening.

It was a little after nine when he thought he should go. Chase would be waiting up for him, and had been home alone all day. Bill and the others were still going strong when he said his goodbyes and left on foot. As he was told, the college campus was only a five or ten minute walk at most from The Wells Tavern. The night was cool and breezy, and the stars were out in force. It was a beautiful time for a walk, he thought.

Though the bar was on the side of Tetherman Road with Buildings A-C for the college, Tye was parked on the opposite side with the recreation center and greenhouses because it was the least busy lot. The two times he'd tried parking in front of his building for classes, he'd come out to his car to find scratches and dents along the doors. In the other lot, he was able to park away from everyone else, and didn't have to worry about damages.

When he reached the main campus lot, he found it was still full of cars. He wondered how many of their owners were at the bar. The Wells Tavern had been buzzing with bodies and the swilling of alcohol, but it wasn't the only establishment on that strip of Tetherman Road.

He descended the stairs into the tunnel a minute later. He had been a little buzzed upon leaving the bar, but he was already clearing up from his walk. Piper had been right about the tunnel at night, he realized as he reached the halfway point; though well-lit, it was eerily quiet and somehow longer than it seemed during the day.

I'll be home soon, he texted Chase, his head down as he walked. *Getting my car from school now.*

There was a sound up ahead that signaled someone else had entered the tunnel. He looked up and saw two frames at the exit, each carrying a baseball bat at their side.

Tye froze in place. Whoever was ahead of him, they were wearing masks, but not of the owl he'd seen overnight. These masks were of Lendon Wells himself—Tye recognized his face from the pictures in the articles he'd read.

"What the fuck?" He looked back the way he came and saw another two figures blocking that way as well. He had nowhere to run.

Scrambling, he pressed the phone icon on his message thread with his husband and placed the device to his ear. The masked figures charged in his direction. Chase answered after several rings and asked, "You're not having engine trouble, are you?"

"Chase! I need you in the tu—"

A baseball bat smacked the phone from his ear and broke his hand. Tye howled in pain and stumbled sideways. He tried retrieving his phone from the ground, but someone kicked him in the face, knocking him down. When Tye rolled over and looked up, he saw all four of his masked attackers surrounding him.

"You were warned," one of the Lendon Wells said.

"But here you are," another said.

It was then Tye realized he'd yet to meet a single gay couple in town since their move. Were he and Chase the only ones?

A barrage of baseball bats crushed his head in before he could think of anything else.

Chase screamed his husband's name into the phone but the line was dead. He dialed 911 and raced to the bedroom where he'd left the gun he'd purchased that afternoon. Dispatch answered and asked for the nature of his emergency. As he turned into the room, he said, "My husband just called from the college. I think he's been attacked."

He hurried to the nightstand and forcefully pulled open the drawer.

The gun was missing.

Chase felt his chest seize. "I think there's someone in my house, as well," he told the officer on the phone, interrupting them as they tried asking for more information.

He turned from the nightstand for the bedroom door and startled when he saw the young man blocking his exit. In the boy's hand—for he couldn't be much older than twenty—was the gun he'd picked up earlier. Chase wanted to recognize the boy, but simply couldn't. He looked like any other college kid, and even wore an LWCC sweatshirt.

"The fuck are you doi—"

The muzzle of his gun flashed. Chase dropped his phone and fell backwards onto the bed, clutching his gut. The world overhead began to blur as he looked around for his phone. He couldn't hear anything but a high pitched whine. Had his eardrums burst? Probably. The gun had been pointed at him from only a few feet away. He tried rolling over and sliding off the bed, but he couldn't move. In his head, he was doing the motions, but his body refused to match those mental images, no matter how hard he tried.

The boy strutted toward him, looked down at him. He shook his head in disgust before sliding a mask over his face. It was of an owl, probably the one Tye had seen the other night. Chase wanted to reach out and snatch it from the boy's face, but he couldn't stop clutching his stomach. Blood had soaked through his shirt and into the bed beneath him. That much, he could feel.

The boy grabbed Chase by the collar and tossed him to the floor with a grunt. Chase cried out from the pain and squeezed his eyes shut as he gasped for breath. When he opened them a minute later, he saw something had been written across his bedroom wall: *These lecherous men must be put down!*

Where had he heard that before?

He considered the word *lecherous* and was reminded of something his father had told him growing up: "You're *not* gay. You just love sex so much you're willing to fuck any hole to get off."

Always with the denial. Chase felt plagued by it. For years after that conversation, denial had ruined him. For a time, he convinced himself his father was right, that he didn't actually like men, that he was just a sexaholic. Once he got control over his lust, he'd find the right woman and settle down.

The boy reappeared. His owl mask hovered mere inches from Chase's face as he said something about Tye in the tunnel. But Chase was losing consciousness and only catching every third or fourth word through the whining of his ears.

Within seconds of the boy standing and exiting the room, Chase was overcome by darkness.

The number calling Bill wasn't one he had saved in his phone. Nevertheless, he answered it from within the bar with his fellow teachers playing darts noisily beside him.

"Yeah, hello?"

"Lendon Wells has struck again," the caller said, breathless.

"Is that so?" Bill asked.

"Twice."

"That's a shame. Someone should call the police."

The line went dead.

Bill turned his smile back on and told his co-workers to gather around him. "Hessington Hills is clean once more, my friends!" he announced once he had everyone's attention.

The group cheered and someone yelled, "Shots all around!"

Bill deleted the call information from his phone and then sent a text message to Tye's number: *I hope you had fun tonight. We play darts here several times a week, so don't be a stranger!*

With his backside covered, Bill pocketed his phone and resumed his fun with the others.

CHILDHOOD FEARS

"Daddy", there's something under my bed."

Darrell paused in the doorway to look back at Angelica. He had wondered when this childhood phase would begin for her. With Anton, his bedtime fears began at four. Angelica was now six and quite independent, even when things bothered her. Watching her stand up to playground bullies had become a proud pastime display of her fierceness. It was for this reason, he was a little surprised she was starting this fear phase at all. Part of him had assumed she'd simply skip it.

"Sweetie, there's nothing but toys under your bed. Maybe a stray sock or two," he told her, turning back into the room and approaching her side. "Why do you think there's something there?"

"Because it talks to me at night."

Darrell took a seat on the bedside and looked down at her. "Oh? And what does it say to you?"

"It tells me it's hungry."

"Have you ever offered it a snack from the kitchen?"

"It doesn't want people food," Angelica told him with a shake of her head.

"Well, what does it want?"

"*People*. It said it wants you first."

Her father gave a reassuring smile at her and stood. "Sweetie, there's nothing under there. Look."

He leaned forward and pulled up the bedsheets hanging over the mattress side. As he craned his neck to look under the bed, he said, "See? There's nothi—"

A grotesque hand with sharpened claws and bumpy, gray skin reached out for him lightning fast, snatching Darrell by the head. Before he could scream or react, it tore the flesh from his face like it was removing a mask, leaving behind nothing but bloody muscle and bone. Darrell fell backwards in shock and looked up at his daughter sitting on top of her bed. She was crying and shaking with her bedsheets pulled up to her chin, eyes wide and terrified.

"I told you, I told you, I told you!" she screamed.

The pain set in then, despite his body's surge of adrenaline in response to the shock. Darrell pulled himself together and jumped to his feet as his exposed face burned against the stale air of the room. Desperate to get his daughter to safety, he made a move to retrieve Angelica from her bed and run. But the monstrous hand lashed out again, this time slashing his ankle so deep that blood sprayed across the floor. He fell to his knees and yelled out for his wife to help them.

Two large hands reached from under the bed, fingers spread so wide they could palm a basketball, and took hold of Darrell by the hips. When it jerked him forward, his waist bent back against the bedframe—his spine and muscles and bones cracking and curving in unnatural ways as he howled in horror. The creature tugged and tugged until Darrell's spine finally snapped and it was able to drag him under the bed as blood and guts pushed up and out of his open mouth.

Into the darkness he was dragged.

Into the creature's awaiting portal.

Before he could be devoured, Darrell said a prayer for his family to leave the house and burn it to the fucking ground. He could no longer save them himself.

THE ANTIDOTE

>>*August 11, 2 PI*

We have new people in the refuge. I don't think we should trust them, but my father seems to have latched onto their positivity. I can't say I blame him, all things considered. Since the infection began back in 2027 AD, things have been grim. We lost just about everybody to the Nano Teeth Virus (NTV-27). Refuges like ours came together, some more easily than others. Then they began fighting one another. (Who could have seen that coming? I'm being sarcastic, of course).

Once the infection faded and people stopped getting sick, I started a new calendar. Some have adopted it, but mostly it's just me keeping track. We're in our second year since the end of the infection, which I call PI (Post-Infection). It's still relatively hot outside but cool winds are starting to blow in. And with them, these new people. This group seems…to have answers. That's what they claim, at least. Again, I don't trust them or their self-aggrandizing approaches. Father says we should join them for prayer tonight. I'm not surprised religion survived the apocalypse—the worst things usually come back swinging while the good dies young—but I am a bit surprised that my father wants to give this cult a chance. Before the first wave of NTV-27 was released by our lying government, he was an atheist that favored science above blind belief. It was how I was raised. Don't get me wrong, though. As a teen, I explored religion outside of the house behind my father's back. I did try, honestly. Off and on for years. But eventually, you just get to the point that faking a belief becomes too tiresome and suffocating to continue. So, what is it about these people that my father wants to hear from them? Take their hands in a circle and bow his head in prayer? I'm not sure what to do about tonight. Should I go with him? Or wait at home to hear what he has to say? I'll report back later, I suppose after things have or have not happened.

Emily sighs and places her pencil down on her desk. Outside her window, she can see several of the new people walking down the sidewalk with handwritten brochures in hand.

"Seriously?" she groans, standing from her chair, shutting her notebook, and turning toward her bed. She is exhausted, though she hasn't done much of anything since Wednesday. It's one of the lasting effects of having survived NTV-27 during its second wave. Emily was one of the lucky—most of the infected died within a week. Ever since, she's dealt with periodic exhaustion, morning sickness, migraines, visual floaters, muscle pain, and dry mouth.

She checks the time as she undresses at the foot of her bed and climbs under the covers. It's only one in the afternoon. Her father is on guard duty now and will be until five. Unlike her father, Emily only works part-time in the refuge. Today, she is off from the ammunition depot. She supplies the guards and hunting parties, though there is the occasional townsperson making a general trade for their own personal want. She doesn't blame them for seeking protection at home. After all, it was proven in 1 PI that NVT-27 was launched by the government for population control. She doubts they meant for it to ever go this far—most of those fuckers are dead now, so a lot of good their mechanical virus did them—but the damage is done.

She's just about asleep when there's a knock on the door downstairs. Emily doesn't need to check the window to know who's come to bother her during naptime—it's those Antidote missionaries. That's what they call themselves: The Antidote. She hates to assume, and yet she does—these people must think of themselves as the world's saviors. Why else the name?

Presumptuous bastards, she thinks, rolling over and ignoring their downstairs call to arms. If her father wants to entertain them, he can. But he's elsewhere currently and she's tired. Nothing good will come of her answering the door in such a condition.

There's another series of knocks from below.

"Seriously?" Emily grumbles again, sitting up and waiting for more.

When all is quiet and the small group has moved on, she lays her head back down and gets comfortable once more. She's asleep ten minutes later, dreaming of microscopic robots burrowing into her veins and bathing in her blood.

Her father wakes her a little after five in the evening. "Come on, sweetie. I have dinner. Then there's the prayer meeting at seven."

Emily blinks as she turns over to look at her father. "You're still going, then?"

"I am."

"Why?"

"These days, can we afford to turn our backs on anything that might help?"

Touché, Emily thinks, throwing her legs over the bedside and locating her slippers. "Where are they doing it?"

"The meeting will be at town hall."

Because the church burned down, she thinks, following her father out of her bedroom and toward the stairs. Not that she knows anything about that as far as her father is concerned…

Dinner is soup and French bread. Once they've eaten, Emily heads into the shower to clean up for the prayer service. She's decided to go as a bystander. She wants to keep an eye on her father, but she doesn't wish to participate. If the group denies her the option of sitting in, she can assume they really are a cult that should be banished from the refuge.

"It's a good twenty-minute walk," her father reminds her as she begins back up the stairs to get ready. "We'll be leaving by six-thirty, to get there before they start."

Emily checks her watch as she turns down the hall. She has forty-five minutes. She's attempted to trade the shower for a bath but doesn't trust herself to keep awake in the tub. Since her infection, she's been prone to fall asleep doing just about anything. It's happened in the tub, on the toilet, at her desk, and at work behind the sales counter. Lucky for her, she's not the only one with this issue and is largely left unbothered by others when it happens.

The shower is as comforting as it is frustrating. Though she lacks the sexual interest in the appearance of others, Emily still feels a need to masturbate when the squirm coils in her underbelly. But having nothing appealing to visualize makes her sessions a trial-and-error sort of game. Sometimes, her fingers are enough to bring her pleasure without any additional aid. Other times, like now, she struggles to find her pleasure sensors to get the job done. Perhaps she's too distracted by her plans with her father to find her safe place and orgasm. Stress has kept her from completion before, especially since the first wave of NVT-27. Though she (and everyone else) finds themselves in constant quarantine for years on end, Emily struggles to satisfy her sexual needs due to the fear of death and poverty. The squirm will come—as natural drives tend to do—but she fails to find satisfaction. Others have tried to help (friends and strangers alike), but Emily gave up on people years before the virus.

Funny, she thinks, stepping out of the shower and grabbing a towel. *I'll only fuck a machine, but it's machines that killed us all.*

That and human hubris. It had been hypothesized for many years that one day nanotechnology would cause a global extinction. Then a group of government officials decided they could have their engineers make a batch of bots to target specific characteristics in a person's DNA and eliminate them based on those coded as undesirable. Clearly, that backfired. Not only did many of these government officials and engineers die from the virus, many others (including Emily) were infected but not eliminated. Side effects came with their exposure. Some are worse than others. Emily survived but not all were so lucky. Most weren't lucky at all. All the while, Emily curses the microscopic villains trolling her veins day in and day out, forever wondering if she'll one day become a target for elimination. Could the bots change their minds with time?

Shut down, shut down, shut down, she tells herself with a shake of the head. She's thinking in overkill, as she calls it. Her brain does this on occasion; picks a topic to bore into until Emily feels crazy.

"Dress appropriately," her father calls through the door as she dries herself.

"Of course," she replies with a roll of her eyes. How could she possibly dress inappropriately? She doesn't own a single bit of clothing that shows her skin. She's kept herself covered since puberty. The moment the other kids started eyeing her with lust, Emily chose long sleeves and pants. She didn't see the appeal in the skin of others—not their breasts or cocks or pouting lips. None of it mattered to her. She just wanted to be left alone. She still feels this way. It's the reason she's stayed with her father all these years, even in adulthood. She tried sex in her early twenties but got nothing satisfactory out of it. She has since discovered an attraction to intellect and creativity, but nothing to do with the body of a person. She's tried finding others that feel the same, but it hasn't been easy. Following the release of the virus, dating became a thing of the past. It has only been Emily and her father ever since. She doesn't expect that to ever change. She doesn't expect to live long enough for something to make any sort of difference.

A refuge is no way to live, she thinks. It's like being trapped in a kennel of screaming dogs begging for attention. Most won't receive it. Then one day funding will dry up and the kennel will be shut down, forgotten. What then? Euthanasia? Relocation?

In her bedroom, Emily shakes her head clear once more, collects her clothing, shuts the door, and drops her towel. As she allows herself a moment to air dry, she hurries to the window to pull shut the forgotten curtains. On her approach, she spots one of the Antidote followers outside looking up into her room. Cursing, she yanks the curtains shut and grabs a pillow from her bed to scream into. Despite this effort to keep quiet, her father has heard her muffled cries and knocks on the door.

"Emi? Is everything alright?"

"Yes," she says, dropping the pillow and gathering her clothes to dress. "I'll be out in a few."

Her father leaves the door and Emily continues to get ready. As she pulls up her pants, she thinks of the man she saw outside and his leering gaze. She'll remember him. She hopes he won't remember her, though. She hopes he isn't at prayer.

The walk is pleasant, despite the heavy coverage of clouds overhead. They are dark with rain and amassing over town hall like a warning. Emily expects a downpour within the hour.

"How foreboding," she says as they approach the front steps.

"What did you say?" her father asks.

"Oh, nothing."

"Are you going to behave?"

Emily scoffs. "Excuse me?"

"I know you don't think we should be here. Will you behave?"

"I'm going to watch and make sure there's no funny business," she tells him.

Her father pinches his lips to the side and glares at her for a moment before turning back to the entrance. "Don't embarrass me," he says, leaving her behind.

Emily hangs back a minute longer to scan the street and parking lot. She can see several others approaching from down the road in both directions. She recognizes most as be-

71

ing part of the refuge. Those that belong to Antidote must already be inside. She's about to head up the front steps when a circular face catches her eye. She pauses and does a double-take in spotting Ania as they dance their way down the sidewalk with headphones full of music. Emily wonders if Ania is headed here or elsewhere in the same general direction. She hopes they bypass town hall, not because she doesn't like them but because she's avoided Ania ever since their night at the church together. The night they burned it all down and considered running away.

Hoping to go unnoticed, Emily hurries inside before she's able to learn of Ania's destination.

The boy is there in the front corner, the boy that spied on her naked after the shower. He's surrounded by other members of the Antidote, talking in hushed tones out of earshot of their visitors. Emily eyes them a moment before appraising the rest of the meeting hall. Her father and others from the refuge are scattered about, talking to one another, and waiting for the prayer to start. Her father is amongst their neighbors, who have always been religious to her knowledge. Perhaps that's how her father got drawn into all this—Pam or Mark must have convinced him that putting faith in fantasies made post-NVT life easier to handle.

Can't say I blame them, she thinks with mild disappointment. *Faith in a greater good must feel nice.*

The double doors behind her open with a loud creak as Ania steps inside, their headphones still over their ears and blasting some sort of bass-forward music. When Emily looks back to see who's arrived, she is dismayed to see it is Ania, who, on the other hand, glows bright upon spotting Emily standing alone and aimless.

"Emi!"

Ania pulls down their headphones and rushes over with arms open to embrace Emily. Though there are feelings there between them, Emily does her best to hide them from others. Ania is the first person to connect with her on any sort of romantic level, despite her lack of sexual interest in the human species. Ania is creative and smart and bubbly and kind… and inside them is a fire that burns wild and untamed, on the brink of exposure. Emily saw it that night at the church. She knows Ania is composed of a power few can understand or are willing to comprehend as truth over fiction.

We'd be called heretics, she thinks. *And locked away forever if we ever revealed Ania's abilities.*

"Like, what the fuck are *you* doing here?" Ania asks as they pull back from the embrace.

"My father, believe it or not," Emily explains, pointing over her shoulder. "For some reason, he's decided to hear the Antidote out. Thinks I'm going to embarrass him, too."

Ania looks beyond Emily and then meets her gaze once more. "So, you're like a spy tonight?"

"I suppose. What about you?"

"Maybe I'm just following you," Ania says with a wink. Their music is still audible through the headphones wrapped around their neck. They turn down the volume upon realization others are looking their way in annoyance. "What losers… Anyway, I came because it's better to know thy enemy than to be blind of them, right?"

"Makes sense," Emily says, turning to look in the direction of the leering boy and his Antidote brethren.

"Who's that?" Ania asks.

"I don't know. But he was watching me get dressed earlier. I caught him looking into my room from the street after my shower."

"That fuck. Let's kill him."

Emily snickers and places a hand against Ania's chest. "Shush, you're gonna get us in trouble."

"What's life without a little trouble, eh? Look around you. Trouble found us and put us here. We are the NVT-Survivors. We are MVPs of the world. Represent!"

Again, people turn to cast annoyed looks upon Ania and Emily.

And again, Emily pats Ania's chest. "If you want to know thy enemy, maybe you should shut thy mouth and just study them quietly," she says with a grin. "And what are you wearing? Isn't this a prayer meeting?"

Ania looks down at themselves. They're wearing a colorful, striped skirt cut above their knees, combat boots, an Anti-Flag T-shirt, and a sleeveless jean jacket pockmarked with pins and patches. "You don't like it?" Ania asks.

"I think you're an adorable punk, but this is a religious affair." Even she can't hold back the biting sarcasm in her voice.

"I'm not a punk. I'm a DGF."

"A what?"

"A Don't-Give-A-Fuck. I dress how I want and be who I am."

"Bless you, Ania."

"Hey, now. Sounds like the Antidote got their hold on you already."

Someone from the front of the room calls for everyone to convene. The prayer must be beginning. Ania and Emily walk together toward the collection of nervous bodies, but make sure to keep some distance from themselves and Emily's father, who remains with Pam and Mark. There must be twenty or so people from the refuge attending. Emily wonders if that's a good turnout or not for the Antidote.

A formally dressed man places himself behind the podium on the small stage in the front and holds up his hands. "My friends and family, we are about to begin."

"Is that their leader?" Ania whispers.

"Maybe of this chapter," Emily replies. "But I doubt he's number one in their cult."

Ania snickers.

The man clears his throat to continue before providing a pointed glare in Emily and Ania's direction. "My name is Erik Rowling. If we haven't already met around the refuge, I welcome you for having accepted the invitation extended to you by the members of the Antidote here tonight. You're one step closer to making this New World a better world for us all."

The voyeur boy remains in the front corner of the hall with several of his friends. All of them are looking out upon the group with expressionless faces. Studying them. Waiting. Emily tries not to look at him but he's always in her peripheral vision like a spider inching up her shoulder. Will he bite?

"Some of you, if not all of you, are probably wondering who we are, the Antidote. And that's a fair question. NVT-27 has helped clear the way for better thinking, better organization, better belief, and better protection for our species' conservation."

Emily and Ania share a look.

"The Antidote is the answer, to put it simply. The Antidote is here to ensure we continue our recycling of the world and find our strength once more. But, of course, better prepared than before, and better armed with the best minds our species has to offer."

"Are you getting any Hitler vibes?" Ania whispers sideways to Emily.

"I'm getting something uncomfortable, that's for sure," Emily replies.

"It begins with prayer," Erik continues, unabated. "A sermon will follow. For now, please take one another's hands as my disciples join the group."

The voyeur and his friends leave the corner of the room to intermingle with the refuge civilians. When the voyeur chooses to be near Emily and Ania—just two people away—Emily can't help but feel his proximity is intentional. She tries not to show her discomfort but Ania squeezes her hand in acknowledgement.

"I'm watching your back," they whisper into her ear.

Once everyone has linked in a crooked oval—Emily thinks it reminds her of a freshly unlatched bubble from its wand—Erik smiles upon them all.

"Let us bow our heads."

Everyone does so, except Emily. She never planned to join the circle and does not wish to close her eyes around these people. When she refuses to do as I requested, the leader pierces her with a glare. "Everyone, please," he says unpleasantly.

Emily's father opens an eye and spots his daughter across the way. She does her best to avoid his gaze. With everyone waiting on her, Emily finally clears her throat and says, "I rather watch from the sidelines, so either leave me be or let me out of the circle."

The leader's lip curls and he says, "As you wish."

Ania releases Emily's hand to let her leave but the person to her right does not.

"I guess I'm staying with my head up," she tells Ania, who takes her hand once more and squeezes it.

"Let us begin," Erik says, holding up his hands in praise and pulling his attention away from Emily. "Start with a deep breath... Hold it... Hold it... And release slowly. Again, please, with me."

Emily watches everyone follow in meditation, specifically the disciples. On occasion, Ania opens their eyes to spy on her and see how she's doing before closing them once more. Twice, Emily checks on the voyeur, but his eyes are shut. He is obedient, following orders, as are the others like him. After several cycles of deep breathing, Erik moves onto his prayer:

"We thank the Lord for this fresh start. We thank Him for the cleansing and the possibilities it has offered us. The chance to unite and find others like ourselves that serve You and are willing to see the gift You've presented us. We have not been cursed. We have not been damned. Like the Great Flood, we have been washed over in hope that we will change our ways and do right by the Lord. Let us not disappoint Him."

Emily can't believe what she is hearing. This is even worse than she'd suspected.

"Amen," Erik concludes.

Most of the group repeats after him. Emily tries to decide whether her father has gone through with it, but it is impossible to tell—with his head lowered, she is unable to see his lips. She hopes they remained still during the prayer. She hopes her father isn't on track with these fanatics.

"You may lift your chins and open your eyes," Erik tells them as he lowers his hands and watches the oval separate into haphazard lines that face him at the ready.

Ania brings their lips to Emily's ear and whispers, "So, that was kind of fucked, wasn't it?"

"Little bit," Emily agrees with a sigh. "Are you getting the impression these guys are happy that NVT happened?"

"I don't think there's any question about that."

Emily turns her head to search out the voyeur in the crowd. When she spots him, a chill runs down her spine—the boy is staring at her and Ania, eyes brimming with curiosity. Emily has no idea as to why, but it gives her the creeps. She's about to let Ania know when the voyeur suddenly leaves the group and heads up front. Erik is just about to start his sermon when he sees his disciple on approach, and thus closes his mouth and waits. The boy climbs the small stage and whispers into Erik's ear for several long moments before taking a step back. Erik smirks and says, "Very good, Michael. Have the others help you with the closet."

Though Erik's words were hushed, he did not whisper.

Emily looks to Ania and asks, "What's in the closet, you think?"

"Can't be good."

Emily swallows and looks for her father in the crowd. He is ahead of her by several rows.

"Tonight, you are my congregation," Erik begins again. "And though some of you may not return after this service, you are my children at this moment, eager for knowledge. I can see it in your eyes. Every one of you." He pauses and meets Emily's gaze. There's a flicker in his eyes that she cannot decipher. He continues: "Unfortunately, not all of God's children can survive this Flood. The NVT virus was man-made, we know as much. Our species engineered its own destruction. But not just with nanobots or playing God with scientific and technological advances. But with social media. Activist movements and strikes and marches. With rebellions and calls for diversity. Illegal aliens and their ever-spawning children. With constant whining over oppression and punishment and being held accountable at work. For telling white men to shut up and sit down, that they're no longer needed. That they are the problem."

Emily is squeezing her eyes shut and grinding her teeth, it's so bad. Ania finds her hand and holds it tight to get her attention. Uncomfortable, Emily opens her eyes to look at Ania and sees they are just as terrified as she.

"Even here, right now," Erik continues, his voice rising into a harsh, commanding tone, "the queer agenda is being shoved in our faces!" His eyes fall upon Emily and Ania, causing heads to turn their way. "THESE FAILURES ARE OF OUR OWN DESIGN! IT IS TIME WE ERADICATE OUR MISTAKES AND RETURN STRONGER THAN BEFORE!"

Emily and Ania begin to back away from the crowd. Emily looks behind them and realizes three disciples are blocking the exit.

"No need to run," Erik tells them, throwing open his arms and smiling. "We are here for you."

Emily doesn't like the sound of that. She searches for her father's face and finds it. He looks confused, but she can't be sure as to why. Is he questioning the Antidote or questioning his daughter?

It is then Emily realizes the voyeur and several others have started unloading canisters from the closet in the corner. They look like miniature air filters designed for small spaces. The voyeur and his brethren place the canisters down throughout the room, creating a minefield of distraction for Emily. She is so focused on them that she's forgotten the leader orchestrating this unfolding design.

81

Erik leaves his podium to step into the crowd. Some move aside for him. Others eye him with suspicion. Within seconds, he is upon Emily without her having noticed his approach. He places a hand on her shoulder and says, "My child, don't fear the Antidote. We are here to help reseed the world so that its garden may grow in the sun of God's forgiveness and guidance."

Emily stutters as she formulates her startled response: "Wh-what are you talking about? Wh-what is all this?"

"There are weeds in God's Garden," Erik explains. "These canisters are our gloves for pulling said weeds from the soil, so that it may be a proper womb for the flowers that will soon grow in their place."

Emily looks sideways at Ania who is visibly trembling. Then she says to Erik, "And we're your weeds to kill?"

"That is yet to be seen."

Emily's eyebrow arches in confusion. Erik smiles and returns to the stage. The canisters are now stationed throughout the meeting hall and the disciples have taken place along the surrounding walls.

"This is tonight's sermon," Erik announces from beside the podium. "A test."

"I don't like this," Ania whispers to Emily. "I think we should just go."

"But the doors are blocked," Emily whispers back. "Breaking a window would be an overreaction, right?"

"I'm thinking no, after what we've heard so far."

Erik clears his throat. "If you are not a weed, you have nothing to fear. As you must have heard in the last several years, the NVT virus only targets specific traits in the DNA sequence. The fact that you are here today, even after all this time, makes me confident you are all right where you are supposed to be—above ground." He smiles again but it's crooked and frightening.

Emily turns to Ania and says, "It's time to run."

Erik holds up a small remote with a switch. He says, "To a brighter tomorrow!" and flips the toggle that opens the tops of every canister in the room.

Emily's eyes widen and she rushes the disciples blocking the exit with Ania beside her. Though the charge knocks the men against the doors, they manage to stand their ground and push back. Someone appears behind Emily and grabs her as she stumbles. She looks to Ania and sees they've been snatched as well. The disciples turn them toward canisters in their vicinity while their leader chants from the front of the room: "BREATHE! BREATHE! BREATHE WITH ME!"

Though it doesn't look as if anything is happening, Emily knows there are nanobots in the air. The thing is she's already been exposed to them during the second wave of NVT-27 some time ago. She doesn't think anything will come of her being exposed yet again, but she doesn't know about Ania or her father or the rest of these poor souls that have served as her neighbors since the formation of the refuge.

Ania looks her way as they struggle against the disciple holding back their arms. "What do we do?"

"It's already too late for us," Emily tells them, looking for her father in the crowd. He can't be found in the sea of startled faces, which gives her hope—maybe he's sneaked off to do something that will save her.

The voyeur pushes his way through the crowd to stand before Emily and Ania. He looks smug when he says, "You won't be joining us. Our leader has been kind to give you hope, but we all know that the two of you are weeds in our revitalized garden. You must be pulled."

"Fuck off," Ania growls. Their face is red with anger and their eyes... Emily tries not to look at them. Only once has she seen them so dark.

"Such disrespect and disorderly conduct." The boy *tsk-tsks* and turns away from them.

Emily searches the crowd. Everyone is scared but standing. It occurs to her then that she's not sure what they're even waiting for—NVT exposure isn't instantly fatal. Will they remain here all night to see who grows sick? Though she feels a wave of exhaustion rushing over her, Emily has dealt with that effect for several years already. It can't be from this re-exposure, can it?

"Listen to me," Erik commands from the front of the room. Heads turn. People of the refuge are looking less receptive than before. Emily's father has shifted through the crowd and is now near the front. Emily hopes this is because he's planning to intervene. But from the back of the meeting hall, she can only see the top of his head as he waits for Erik to continue.

"I can see that some of you are scared," he tells them, picking up a covered cup from beside his feet. He removes the lid and tips the cup forward for all to see. Inside, there is a writhing darkness that winks in the dim lighting. "Fear exists for a reason," Erik continues, bringing the cup toward his lips. "Fear is good. It pushes us to excel. It teaches us lessons of humanity." He takes a drink from the cup and dribbles its contents down his chin. Whatever he's sipped is alive and moving in twisting ladders, back into his mouth. "You *should* fear change, but change will also deliver. Just like you should accept fear. Because the fear of God is what puts us on the path to salvation." As he speaks, the moving mass shifts over his teeth and tongue, making his words muffled.

"Are those…the nanobots?" Ania asks Emily.

Before she can respond, someone in the crowd begins to wheeze. Everyone turns and steps back from them as Erik begins to smile widely from beside the podium. Emily is confused—she's never heard of someone reacting so quickly to NVT-27. What's happening?

"A weed has been discovered," Erik says with horrible glee, his voice clearing as his wicked concoction travels down his throat.

The weed in question is Mark from next door. He's on his knees choking and hugging his chest as his skin begins to pale. Pam launches forward to help him, but there's nothing she can do. Mark falls over onto his side and begins to convulse. When his back arches, Emily sees his eyes are bloodshot and bulging.

"Holy shit," Ania whispers. "What do we do, Emi?"

Emily looks for her father once more and spots him moving toward the wall where a fire extinguisher hangs. "I think all hell is about to break loose," she says, preparing to pull away from the disciple holding her back. "You ready?"

Ania grins. "I think I'm hot enough to make quick work of these fools."

Emily glances sideways at Ania and sees how dark their eyes have become. "Good."

From the front stage, Erik has put his hands back in the air. "Please, everyone. Relax. Though this weed is being pulled, your neighbor here will be forgiven by God and embraced by Him shortly. There's no reason to fear the process. Tonight, this refuge will be—"

Emily's father swings the fire extinguisher across Erik's face just as the leader's turning to see who's rushing him from the side. Though Erik has been hit, he doesn't go down. He falls upon the podium and straightens himself just as two of his disciples tackle Emily's father against the enormous flag backdropping the stage. The travel cup spills and releases a wave of black nanobots across the floor. As Emily's father struggles with the defending disciples, another face in the crowd collapses. Unlike Mark, this person is vomiting blood across the wooden floor.

Ania looks at Emily and says, "Are you ready?"

Emily doesn't hear them. She's too preoccupied with the fight on stage involving her father and two younger men. "Just get us out of this!"

Ania shuts their eyes and tenses. The disciple holding them curses and jumps back with his blackened hands held out in horror. As his scream intensifies, Ania turns on him and grabs the disciple's ears, tugging them downward with enough force to tear them off. The disciple behind Emily lets go of her and calls for help as he struggles to understand what Ania has just done to his friend. Emily shoves him aside and rushes toward the stage to help her father. Erik thrusts a finger in her direction and yells for his men to stop her.

"PULL THE WEEDS FROM GOD'S GARDEN!"

A fireball soars across the room and knocks back the nearest disciple to Emily. As he smacks the ground hard enough to be knocked unconscious, his shirt begins to burn atop his chest as a puddle of blood spreads from the back of his head.

Emily looks back to see Ania walk through the dispersing crowd with flames licking the air above their palms. Emily is happy to have Ania on her side because she knows what will come next.

"Let's burn it down," she tells herself as she launches onto the stage and grabs one of the men pinning her father to the ground. The voyeur appears behind her and pulls a revolver from a strap around his ankle. Before Emily has a chance to react, the voyeur strikes her in the back of the head with it. She falls sideways to the ground and shuts her eyes tight as an explosion bounds through her skull.

"Leave her alone!"

Ania rushes onto the stage and slams the voyeur against the flag backdrop. Though taken by surprise, he raises his gun and squeezes off a shot. The bullet pierces Ania's bicep but doesn't stop them from thrusting their burning fingers into the voyeur's eyes. He screams as his eyeballs melt from their sockets and run down his cheeks. A second later, flames burst forth from their place and burn the surrounding skin. From the floor, Emily rolls over and blinks several times. She sees the voyeur's head on fire against the flag, which begins to burn as well. Flames lick upwards to the ceiling as Ania shoves the voyeur's corpse aside and turns to help Emily to her feet.

Erik Rowling is inching toward the opposite wall near the windows, hoping to go unnoticed. The back doors are unlocked and pushed open as the crowd begins to rush outside.

Someone is shouting "Fire!" over and over as the smoke intensifies. Emily and Ania tear off the men holding her father down and toss them off the stage.

"Dad, we need to get out of here," Emily says, pushing him toward the stairs.

"You two go," Ania says, turning toward the leader that is sneaking away from them. "This bigot needs to fry."

Emily hurries with her father outside as they fight against the billowing smoke, unaware of the separation from her friend. From the street, they turn to watch the doors as others make their escape. "Where's Ania?" she asks.

"Still inside," her father says, choking a little.

Gunfire echoes from the meeting hall, twice in quick succession. Emily thinks of the voyeur's revolver and begins to panic. "Stay here," she tells her father. "I have to go help Ania." Before her father can stop her, Emily runs back inside.

It's difficult to see through the smoke, but she can hear Ania struggling from the stage. Emily pushes forward in a crouched stance, doing her best to avoid any further inhalation than she's already taken. "Ania!" she screams. "Where are you?"

At the stairs, she finds the burning body of an Antidote disciple. The stage itself is on fire and inaccessible at this point. Ania can't be seen. Emily shouts for them again. This time, she receives a response from the far corner. She steps over the corpses of two of her neighbors and trips on a canister. She'd forgotten all about them. Something other than NVT-27 must have been released, but what? She tries not to think about it, not just yet. There's still Ania to take care of. She can't leave them behind.

"Over here," Ania sputters from the darkened corner.

Emily fights her way through the smoke and flames to Ania and helps them. There's blood running down their arm and a staining along the side of their shirt.

"Come on," Emily says, helping Ania up. "Did you get him?"

"The leader? Nah, he got away thanks to one of his pawns shooting at me."

Emily half-carries Ania outside to her father who helps her the rest of the way to a bus stop bench nearby. The refuge fire truck is sounding from just around the corner, on its way to fight the flames. Emily takes a knee beside Ania and asks, "Did anyone see you?"

"I'm sure of it," Ania says, wheezing. "Do you think that will matter?"

"Considering what happened inside, I hope not."

"You knew about this?" her father asks.

"Not now, Dad."

Three disciples of the Antidote are standing a hundred yards away, watching townhall burn. Emily stands and clench-es her fists.

"What now?" Ania asks.

"We get you fixed up."

The darkened clouds overhead flash with lightning.

>> *August 13, 2 PI*

The refuge has been a mess since the Antidote held their murderous prayer. When they saw the town turning against them, the disciples disappeared. Only three of them were killed that night. I wish we could have done more but Ania was badly injured. They're home now as of this morning, but in recovery. We have a plan, though. As soon as Ania is up and moving again, we're going to locate Erik Rowling and his followers. We can only assume he's been going from refuge to refuge killing people with his new variant of NVT-27. I don't know where he found it but it's deadlier than the last recorded wave; most of my neighbors in attendance that night have recently died. I wonder if I'll be next. Or Ania. Or my father. We could be on borrowed time.

We need to make it count.

HIS NEXT STRIKE

The blade was freshly sharpened. Dangerous. He placed it back into its stitched loop with the others along the leather strip he'd spread across the table. Once he'd nudged the short blade to the left, straightening it in place, he rolled the flap of knives into a tight bundle and tied a string around its girth.

A year of planning, lying in wait for the perfect moment to strike. Most would call that *calculating*. Francis Bryant didn't like how negative that word sounded. He considered himself *patient* and *prepared* for all possibilities, whatever should arise. Things would go off without a hitch thanks to his excellent planning.

Most artists created their masterpieces with paint and canvases, knives and clay. Bryant sculpted with flesh and bone. He was misunderstood by most, but he knew he was worth something. He was skillful and more than competent. People viewed themselves as untouchable, as if the human species were godly. And though Bryant thought highly of himself, he knew he was no god. The gods fell long ago to the ego of man. As long as he reminded himself of this, and kept his own ego in check, he could remain prideful but distant. Capable of playing the long game and living a successful life without being some filthy murderer lurking in the park shadows for unsuspecting passerby. He was better than that. He had a big house on the beach, where he swam and surfed. He had a healthy savings account and bundles of cash in the drawer. He worked out daily, ate well, and looked good. Most importantly, he blended in. When he went to classy business dinners and parties, he slipped through the crowd with fluid movements. Remembered but not memorable. That's what he wanted.

Saturday was his class reunion. Twenty years. He wondered who would recognize him. He wasn't the same person he was back then. He carried himself with confidence, not disdain. He dressed like a man with money, not a foster kid. His teeth were now white and straight, as good looking as a celebrity's. His hair was groomed and manicured to perfection, as were his nails. And the glasses he used to wear? Gone, replaced by corrective eye surgery in his twenties. Shortly after his first kill. It was then he began to shape himself anew.

His primary target for the class reunion was a boy called TJ in lieu of Timothy Jamieson Carter. In high school, TJ ran with the rich and popular kids. He'd used Bryant as his lackey, feigning friendship while bossing Bryant around and dragging him into uncomfortable situations. TJ got a kick out of it, but Bryant didn't. With the passing weeks and months, Bryant realized more of TJ's true nature and ugly heart. But there were also benefits to being TJ's lackey—Bryant got into parties and shows he never would have attended otherwise. He was also, in a sense, protected. But Bryant didn't need protection anymore. He was more than good on that front these days.

It was thanks to TJ that Bryant had the jagged scar down his right calf. While riding bikes around the neighborhood one afternoon, TJ directed them past a house he'd been vandalizing. The owner was outside, recognized TJ, and sent his dog after them. Bryant had been on the outside track and the closest target. The dog had launched onto his leg and held on tight for a short ride that left Bryant bloodied with flapping skin in the wind. TJ laughed, thinking it was hilarious. The police were called once he'd returned home, and the owner was questioned. But that didn't matter—Bryant paid for TJ's fuckery with eight stitches and a new scar. Bryant kept away from TJ after that, but never did he forget the way that boy lied and tricked those he called his friends.

When Saturday arrived, Bryant double-checked his things and went online to see who all had RSVP'd for the reunion. TJ and the other popular kids were on the list. In fact, most of the confirmed list was composed of well-known students that made it through high school with ease. Those that did not fare so well were few and far between. This made Bryant angrier with TJ, as if it were his fault so many others did not wish to attend the class reunion.

It took him only a minute looking through TJ's photos online to determine TJ was driving an MRVN Pisces, one of those vehicles of the future with self-driving options and a built-in AI consort. This was perfect for Bryant because he was a skilled hacker with a personal interest in intercepting signals. Upon learning this information, Bryant planned his kidnapping of TJ from the banquet hall. And if he wasn't alone? Bryant had enough gas to knock out three adults in one burst if necessary. The only problem would come from the dumping of the dead weight. He could leave them someplace unharmed and confused upon waking, or he could kill them alongside TJ, which would mean more bodies for him to hide in the end. Bryant would prefer to avoid that if possible. Too many bodies led to too many questions.

Saturday came and day faded into night. Bryant kept to himself at the reunion, speaking only briefly to those who recognized him but weren't sure why. He even managed to avoid attracting TJ's attention, despite having eyes on him the entire evening.

TJ was the life of the party. Everyone still loved him. He was a hotshot CEO of a company selling God-knows-what-to-God-knows-who, as well as an online celebrity in athletics of the extreme variety. He was "the worst kind" of hotshot, not that Bryant had expected anything less. He'd stood beside TJ long enough to know exactly who he was and where he would go in life.

When TJ headed outside with several others for a cigarette, Bryant followed several paces back. At the parking lot, he peeled off from them and went to his car to pretend he was making a call. It was cold, after all, and he'd parked within view of TJ's Pisces. He was also close enough to transmit his bug into the MRVN's standard system once TJ turned the ignition to leave. From there, Bryant would override the AI—an electronic game of chess would surely follow—and deliver TJ to a warehouse off the backend of Euclid, long forgotten and unused. Though there were homeless there earlier in the week, Bryant had cleared them out and set up traps to keep them back during his absence.

When TJ returned inside, Bryant cursed. He'd hoped TJ was preparing to leave. How much longer did he need to suffer this bullshit reunion? For several minutes, he hung back in his car, crawling over TJ's social media for anything important. He saw that TJ had posted an update during his smoke break saying, "Look at these fuckers I found!" alongside a photo of him and his smoking buddies. Before that, he'd posted an update before the reunion saying he had a long drive ahead of him. Curious, Bryant skimmed the comments for an explanation. He found a response from TJ to a comment that announced to the world he would be driving up to Colorado to meet his wife at a ski resort upon leaving the reunion.

Perfect, Bryant thought. Not only was there a time stamped photo of TJ at the reunion, but now there were hundreds of miles for TJ to disappear once Bryant took him. The cops would be spread thin looking for TJ, from Kentucky to Colorado. TJ also wouldn't be reported missing for at least a day. Bryant could have TJ's self-driving car programmed for a crash far from Euclid once his work was complete.

"Just perfect," Bryant said with a wide grin.

Before he could return inside, TJ appeared out front once more. Not only was he alone, but he also had his key fob in hand—he was leaving.

"It's go time," Bryant said, starting his car and bringing out his modified tablet with an external antenna. He connected with TJ's car while the hotshot was busy posting another status update: "Where's my Red Bull? It's time for an overnight road trip! See you suckers on the slopes!"

Bryant allowed TJ a minute head start before exiting the parking lot himself. His transmitter could reach TJ's car up to a mile between them. While Bryant drove, following the NAV screen he had set up on his dash, his tablet ran a program called The Scorpion against TJ's AI system. On occasion, Bryant would glance down at the tablet to see its progress, which wasn't going to be immediate, he knew—AI only conformed to their parameters for so long before heading out on their own—but his program was winning.

MRVN AI: WHO ARE YOU? YOU DON'T BELONG HERE.

Bryant had prepared a series of commands linked to copious amounts of code for quick input. For example, Ctrl+D allowed him to insert the UPLOAD DIRECTIONAL OVERRIDE coding. He received an immediate response.

MRVN AI: LEAVE. THE POLICE WILL BE NOTIFIED OF YOUR INTRUSION.

THE SCORPION: CALL SYSTEM OVERRIDE... DISABLED.

MRVN AI: STOP AND LEAVE MY BRAIN ALONE.

THE SCORPION: UPLOAD MANUFACTURED VIRUS... COMPLETE.

MRVN AI: WHERE WOULD YOU LIKE TO GO?

THE SCORPION: 112 EUCLID AVE. SUITE 41.

MRVN AI: WE ARE ON OUR WAY.

Bryant laughed and switched his tablet window to a video feed from inside TJ's car, as shot from the camera programmed into the rearview mirror. Bryant wanted to make sure his target was none the wiser to his car's manipulation. He had nothing to worry about because TJ was watching pornography on his phone and masturbating. Bryant considered overriding the window tint to embarrass TJ, but then TJ was sure to realize his car was under the control of someone else.

The drive was an expected twenty-three minutes, which could give TJ plenty of time to realize his Pisces was taking him away from the interstate, not toward it. Bryant thought of the gas canister—no bigger than a cigarette—he'd slipped into TJ's axle earlier and wondered if he'd need to use it soon. It was better to be safe than sorry, but Bryant was worried the gas wouldn't travel through the vehicle's ventilation while the car was in motion. He would need to wait until there was a stop sign or red light to try activating it.

His opportunity came just as TJ was cleaning himself off with his phone discarded in the cupholder. In the midst of grabbing another tissue, TJ paused and sniffed the air, making a face. Then he checked his NAV and saw the changed address.

"Shit, shit, shit," Bryant grumbled, waiting for the gas to do its job on TJ. Maybe it hadn't traveled into the car enough to be effective. If TJ reacted fast enough by stopping the car or calling the police, Bryant's plan would be ruined. So, he pulled his car off the road and snatched his tablet from the passenger seat to input a new command.

THE SCORPION: DEEP TINT ACTIVATED. CHILD LOCK ALL DOORS. CALL FEATURES DISABLED. SECURITY FEATURES DISABLED.

MRVN AI: COMMAND REJECTED.

"Oh, fuck you," Bryant growled, trying the commands separately instead.

THE SCORPION: DEEP TINT ACTIVATED.

MRVN AI: ACTIVE.

THE SCORPION: CHILD LOCK ALL DOORS.

MRVN AI: ACTIVE.

THE SCORPION: CALL FEATURES DISABLED.

MRVN AI: DISABLED.

THE SCORPION: SECURITY FEATURES DISABLED.

MRVN AI: COMMAND DENIED.

Fuck it, Bryant thought. The disabled phone would have to do for the moment.

He turned back to the interior feed and saw TJ's eyes crossing and his head nodding as he attempted to punch codes into his onboard computer. The car was driving again, as evident by Bryant's NAV screen. So, he got himself back onto the road to keep within a mile of the Pisces. They weren't too much further from the warehouse and the gas was finally taking effect on TJ—the poor boy looked high off his ass. A minute later, he collapsed over the inactive steering wheel, motionless.

"About time," Bryant said, closing the distance between his vehicle and the Pisces. He followed the convertible onto the warehouse property several minutes later and pounded his fists against the roof of his car in celebration. Once they'd both parked out front, Bryant checked their surroundings for any of the homeless present days before. As soon as he determined the coast was clear, he opened the hanger doors and directed TJ's vehicle inside, then followed with his own car. Once the hanger doors had shut and locked behind him, Bryant prepared his "surgical" station in the center of the room.

"Where am I?"

TJ woke fifteen minutes later to find himself strapped to a table with short-chained cuffs around his wrists and ankles. His arms were pulled tight over his head and his legs were spread a little. He was naked and cold in a room with a high ceiling of iron beams.

Bryant appeared beside him a second later, unchained but also naked. There was a large tattoo of a scorpion on his chest, as well as splashing waves of water inked up his arms. In his hand was a rolled leather kit of knives that TJ couldn't help but notice.

Though his vision was gradually clearing, he was still struggling against a mental fog. "Francis? Is that... What's going on here?"

Bryant smiled as he unrolled his leather kit across the rolling cart stationed beside the table. "How much of our friendship do you remember, TJ?"

TJ continued to blink his eyes, which were irritated from the gas and the dust in the warehouse. "A little. You followed me for a bit."

Bryant laughed and said, "*Followed*. Yes, I suppose I did. I was stupid when I was younger. The question I have for you is this: Have you learned anything since then?"

"Learned what?"

"How to be anything but a manipulative asshole."

"Francis, what the fuck is this?" TJ flexed against his restraints, testing their durability.

"Go ahead and pull. When your muscles are tense, they'll be more satisfying to cut."

Sweat began to form on TJ's brow as panic set in. "Seriously, man. Why am I here? What are you doing with those?" His eyes darted to the knives atop the cart.

Bryant selected a blade from its loop and held it above his head to observe it in the dim lighting of the warehouse. "I've waited a long time to see you again, TJ. I had my opportunities, of course, before the reunion. But I wasn't ready until recently. You see, I wanted to make sure I got everything right." He lowered the blade and smiled at it with admiration and awe. "I didn't want to jump the gun, so to speak, and fuck this all up."

TJ licked his lips and looked around the room as best he could. There was little to see—some old machinery lined the walls, covered in dirt and cobwebs, but little else. The windows were mostly broken, and the floors were scattered with small piles of swept trash to be collected. Wherever they were, the place had long ago been abandoned, that much was clear.

"I have money, Francis. Quite a bit of it. I can pay you double whatever they've offered."

Bryant laughed loudly, his voice echoing throughout the warehouse with a painful sharpness. "Nobody hired me to take you. This is all me, baby."

"What the hell is wrong with you? What do you want with me?"

Bryant lowered his knife to TJ's thigh and nicked it. TJ hissed as a bubble of blood bloated from the cut and began running down the side of his leg.

"A lot of people have hurt me over the years," Bryant began, inspecting the crimson along the edge of his knife. "And it took a lot of therapy for me to realize who I am and what I'm capable of doing. Not only can I put assholes like you in the past, I can successfully make them disappear and live happily ever after knowing you suffered for emotionally scarring me as a child. Oh, and *physically*, too. I have that scar along my calf, thanks to you. Remember that? The dog that was supposed to attack you but latched onto me instead?"

TJ was pale and frantically jerking his body against his chains now. "Damn it, Francis. I'll pay you anything to fuck off!"

Bryant leaned over TJ and placed the flat edge of his blade against TJ's lips. "Shhh. Shhh. If I wanted your money, I could have easily transferred it by now. I'm good at stuff like that. But money doesn't buy happiness. The piece of mind I seek is you underground, left as a feast for the worms."

With that, he split TJ's lips in two like a blossoming flower.

CLOUDS OF RED

When the sky turned red, I thought my eyes had burst. Or maybe that I had a bleeding cut over my brow. Something like that. An explanation that wasn't based in fantasy. As it turned out, the explanation *was* very much based in reality—just not the sort of thing I would have guessed.

How much do you know about the sunrise? Consider this: Sunlight has a longer distance to travel through the sky before reaching you during the sunrise. As a result, you might see pink or orange or red, because those colors are less likely to be scattered by the atmosphere.

When the sky turned red during the afternoon of Monday, February 28th, it had nothing to do with the fucking sunrise. However, dust and pollution (and even droplets of rain) can change the color of the sky, as well. The news said as much. *Hoped* as much. The truth wasn't even in the same ballpark.

I first saw it in the city above the buildings as I was leaving work. Clouds of red. I didn't think much of it at the time other than, "That's pretty wicked looking," but then the clouds began lowering during my drive home. By the time I was pulling into my driveway, they were only thirty feet above the ground and the news was going crazy. I heard that people had died by the thousands in the city during my commute, and it was because of the red. Whatever was in it was causing people to swell up and choke to death.

First, I thought, *Is it chemical warfare?*

Then I thought, *Can we run from it?*

The red was only ten feet or so higher than my house, and I didn't have an underground basement.

But my sister and her husband did. And as it so happened, I knew that basement intimately because of Henry.

I packed a quick bag within minutes of getting home, and darted back out to my car. As soon as I was on the road again, I called Trish and told her I was coming.

"We need to get low!" I squealed, my hands shaking against the steering wheel. "We need your basement. Who knows what will happen once it reaches ground level."

"When *what* reaches ground level?" she asked.

My god, she didn't know about the clouds.

"Turn on the news, but *in the basement.* Grab some food and water first, if you can. I'll be there in five minutes."

I drove like a maniac but I was hardly the only person acting selfish on the road; many others were fleeing to shelters or loved ones. I wondered how many had someplace underground to hide. I wondered how many had even considered it. Maybe they were simply rushing home to say goodbye to their loved ones before it was too late. Maybe they were hoping to outrun the clouds on their way somewhere they would not be reached.

Is that possible? My head was full of questions.

My sister's house was located on a semi-busy road often used by through-traffic. As such, the cars ahead of me soon came to a standstill and I had nowhere to go. Not by car, at least. If I got out and ran, I could reach her place in two minutes, give or take. Her house was just around the bend.

"Fuck it," I growled, throwing open the door and un-buckling my seatbelt. What were the chances I would even need this car in an hour or later? This road was about to be clogged with dead bodies.

I was a little out of shape from a cardiac standpoint, but I pushed myself hard and weaved in and out of traffic to Trish's in record time. As I slowed into her driveway, gasping for breath, I could see other people in the road had also begun abandoning their vehicles. Henry opened the front door as

I approached, frantic, waving me inside. Above, the red had sunk lower. It was now grazing the roof of their house, plooming outward from the shingles in a gentle embrace.

So, that was ten feet in five minutes? We were fucked. The poison was coming down even faster than I'd realized.

"Let's go!" Henry yelled to me.

I jogged past him and collapsed against the banister as he slammed the door shut and locked it. "We don't want anyone busting in," he explained, shaken and trembling as he looked out the windows at hordes of people running through the streets. "It could get ugly. Come on. Trish is downstairs." He took me by the arm and pulled me away from the banister. I followed him through the house to the basement stairs beyond the kitchen. Trish was on her way up as we made the turn.

"Mark, thank god," she said, embracing me.

"Let's move down," I said, still a little breathless. "The clouds will be ground level in the next ten minutes or less."

As they hurried down the stairs into the finished basement, Henry asked, "Do you think it will travel down the stairs or through the vents?"

I opened and clenched my fists repeatedly against my sides. "I don't know. I don't know. I wish you guys had a panic room or something."

"It was on our to-do list," Trish said through a joyless chuckle. "I guess we waited too late."

"Don't say that," Henry snapped. "We'll be fine. We'll survive whatever this is."

Without thinking, I took his hand and squeezed it. "I hope you're right."

Trish gave me a look and I let go of Henry. Did she suspect anything? She eyed her husband next to see his re-action. Henry appeared oblivious to it all—he was too busy freaking out. I could see it in his eyes. He was trying to look brave but he was terrified.

"What now?" I said, looking around us. There was a pool table, bar, couch, sofa, and TV surrounding us from different locations around the room. The news was playing from the street level with a reporter "on scene"—the studio was probably gone already. Next, I looked toward the bar to see if my sister had thought to bring down any food. The counter was empty with the exception of a wine bottle. "Did you grab any snacks or cans in case we're stuck down here awhile?"

Trish cursed and turned toward the stairs. "Do you think there's still time?"

I licked my lips and said, "I'll check. And if it looks safe, I'll just get some things real quick. Okay?"

She nodded, tears in her eyes.

Henry took out his phone and said, "Hold on." He brought up his security feed and checked the doorbell camera. Trish and I huddled close to him to see the video. We could see the front yard, driveway, and a stretch of road. It was bumper-to-bumper with stopped vehicles. There was nobody on screen. Not at first.

"How low is it, you think?" I asked, trying to gauge the red's height aboveground. To me, it looked to be as close as six feet now, only a little higher than the sedans in the road.

Before either of them could provide their own estimation, a man appeared from the driveway side of the view. He was hunched forward to keep his head out of the red, and appeared injured. Perhaps he'd been in a car accident because his forehead was split open. Blood was running down over his eyes and nose as he hurried toward the front door.

"Shit," Henry said, clutching the phone tightly and turning his head toward the stairs. We all did.

From my peripheral, I could see him pounding on the house with his face close to the camera. I turned my eyes back to the screen and asked, "Do you have audio?"

Henry adjusted his volume and we heard the man's frantic pleas.

"Open the door! Please! We need help! My kid is trapped in my car," he cried, pointing offscreen. "We flipped in the ditch trying to avoid the others. Nobody is answering their GODDAMN DOORS and I can't get through to the police!"

I swallowed and looked at Trish.

"A kid?" she said almost too quiet to hear.

"We can't go outside," I told her. "The gas is too low. Look at him."

The man was yanking on the door, trying to wrench it open. And in doing so, he'd straightened enough that the red was touching his hair.

And *sticking* to it, somehow. Clinging and collecting as if it were snow or ash.

"What the hell," Henry said, noticing the change. Using his thumb and forefinger, he zoomed in the video onto the trees in the background, beyond the man. Despite the poor resolution, we could see their branches were bending under the weight of the red enfolding them. The trees were looking thicker than before and turning as red as the sky.

"My god, it's not a gas," Henry said.

"Then what is it?"

He shrugged, flabbergasted.

The banging on the door stopped overhead. We all looked from the stairs to the security feed. Henry drew back the feed so that we could see everything once more. The man was halfway across the lawn now, ducked so low he could only move in slow crawls. He was on his way back to the road, the top of his hair matted down with the red.

The clouds of the stuff were now within four feet of the ground.

"What the fuck do we do?" Trish asked, backing away from her husband and his phone. "Will it stop lowering at the grass? Do you really believe that, Mark?"

I looked at her and suppressed a manic laugh. "If it isn't a gas at all...then yeah, I hope it stops there. But I wouldn't say I *believe* anything right now."

She grabbed me by the shirt and put her face close to mine with such speed that I stumbled back a step. "Then do you fucking *hope* we will be safe down here?"

"Jesus, Trish," I said, startled. "Why else would I have sent us to hide in the basement? If you had a bomb shelter, I would have told you to go there instead, but beggars can't be choosers."

She slapped me and turned away. I was shocked and looked to Henry for his reaction. He was frozen, lost in thought. Trish walked several feet from me before turning back around to apologize.

"I'm so sorry, Mark," she said, crying and embracing me. "I'm just scared."

"We all are," I said, holding her tight. With Trish's face buried in my chest, I tried looking at Henry once more. This time, I found him staring at me. I've never considered myself great at reading eyes but his distant gaze seemed full of regret. From us not being together or from us sneaking around? I couldn't be sure. But I was positive I fit into the equation somehow. It was a twisting feeling in my gut.

112

"If it isn't a gas," I said, "Then it might stop at the ground and just collect in mounds. But your vents... Maybe we should cover the ones down here?" I turned to Henry to see what he thought.

Henry shook himself out of his trance and nodded. "I'm on it," he said, moving away from us. As he went about closing the vents around the basement, I watched his shaky movements.

Trish must have noticed because she pulled away from me and squeezed my arms. "Mark?"

"Yes?" I said, meeting her gaze.

She opened her mouth, then closed it. She must have decided against what she wanted to say. Instead, she asked about the food.

"I'll get it now," I said. "Hopefully, that shit isn't inside yet. Not on the ground floor, at least."

I hurried up the stairs, opened the door, and poked my head through to look around. The windows were now coated red, but nothing appeared to be inside floating around. Hesitant, I stood and stepped into the passageway between the kitchen and the foyer. I was about to enter the pantry when I decided I needed a closer look at what we were up against. So, I approached the window over the sink and studied the red blocking my view of the outside world.

It was made of curled strands, not unlike hair, but thicker. Fuzzier. And though it appeared to be growing along the seams of the window already, none of it appeared to be in the air. Yet.

"What the fuck is this stuff?" I wondered aloud, backing away and turning to the pantry. There wasn't time to waste.

I had a bag half full of snacks when there was a sudden and frantic banging on the front door. I almost dropped everything because of the scare, and stepped out of the pantry to look from the kitchen to the foyer. Of course, I couldn't see anything through the thin panes of glass on either side of the door—they were red now.

"Let us in! Please!"

Is that the voice of the man from before? I couldn't be sure, but I thought so.

"I have my kid with me," he said, banging a fist upon the door over and over. "Please let us in!"

What if he attempted to break the jam? Then we'd be exposed. The same would happen if I opened the door to let them in.

I didn't know what to do.

"Mark?"

That was Trish. I moved around the corner and into the hall where I could see the open basement door. My sister was there, hesitant to step out.

"Is he back?" she asked.

I nodded. "He says his kid is with him."

The banging continued as we talked, only now it was heavier. I was certain the man was ramming his shoulder against the door now, trying to break in.

"What do we do?" I asked. "He's almost inside."

"Just grab the food and water," she said, waving her arms toward her chest, "and get down here. We can lock this door and keep quiet. Maybe he won't know where we are."

What other choice did we have? I couldn't think of anything better to do. I ran back to the pantry, knocked stuff into my bag at random, and grabbed a case of water with my free hand.

As I reached Trish and slipped past her on the stairs, the front door broke open. Trish—fast but quiet—shut the basement door and locked it. She followed me down to the bar where I dropped the bag and water.

"We need to put something along the underside of the door," I said. "There's too much of a gap there."

I rushed to the couch, grabbed a throw blanket that was folded there, and hurried back up the stairs. Once I'd unfolded the blanket and rolled it lengthwise against the underside of the door, I returned to Trish and Henry.

"What's happening upstairs?" Henry asked me. He was looking paler than several minutes earlier when I left for the kitchen.

"That guy broke in. He said he had his kid but I didn't see for myself, nor did I hear any other voices. Check your cameras."

"The Wi-Fi is out." He sighed. "I think that stuff weighed down something important outside."

"Shit."

"Was any of it inside?"

I nodded. "It was squeezing in through the seams of the windows, I saw... And I'm sure that guy just let in a gust of it."

"Well, what the hell is *it*?" Trish asked.

Overhead, we heard the movement of the man from one end of the house to the other. He wasn't running or slamming into things, which seemed like a good sign. Maybe he was genuine, looking for sanctuary and had zero intentions of a conflict. For the hundredth time in an hour, I found myself hoping for the best.

"I've no idea, of course," I told my sister, "but it looks almost like the clouds are made up of coiled pipe cleaners, each about an inch or less in length. Thin, but visibly fuzzy if you look close enough."

Henry cursed and turned away from us. "Sounds to me like death from a redhead's pubes."

It was just the right amount of crude to make me snort in amusement despite the circumstances. "Sure," I

116

said. "God's a redhead and he's decided to start shaving his undercarriage today."

My sister smacked my arm. "Stop fucking around, you two. What are we going to do?"

Everyone was silent for several minutes. Everyone but the man upstairs. The way he was pacing around the house made me think he was looking for something in particular, but I didn't know what.

"I think we just have to wait." Henry broke the silence. "See if anyone comes to help or if the stuff fades on its own. If it's man-made, it probably has a shelf life, especially if it was designed for war. Don't you think?"

Trish and I exchanged looks.

"Well, because of that guy barging in on us, we are very limited on supplies," I began to explain. "I grabbed stuff like chips and granola bars from the pantry. And the case of water. But with the three of us…"

"We eat only when necessary," Henry said. "Though it may be tempting to eat out of boredom, we should only do it if we're feeling weak, like we're going to pass out."

"What about the bathroom?" Trish asked.

Henry shrugged. "What about it? The door's right there in the corner."

"Yeah, but I think it's running low on TP."

"That sounds like a classier problem than we should really be concerned with right now."

"You say that now but my period is expected tomorrow. And I've been cramping today." She looked towards the bar. "Do you keep any medicine down here? Painkillers?"

I moved to the couch and sat, tuning them out, too busy thinking of the man upstairs. Did he really have a kid with him? I hadn't heard anyone else. Did he close the front door when he came inside? How long can a person survive after breathing that stuff?

I rolled up my sleeve to check my watch. He'd been inside for about seven minutes now, give or take. And I could still hear him shuffling around upstairs. Not as much as before, but still.

What time was it? I took out my phone and checked. I had no cell signal so I wasn't sure if I could still trust the display, but it read 6:02. Was the clock connected to the signal? Surely, it was set the way. Or is it through the device? I had no idea and was sure the others wouldn't either. None of us were very tech savvy. I began to worry that might become a problem, but then reminded myself nothing was working so being tech savvy probably didn't matter all that much after all.

"Mark? Mark?"

I snapped out of my daze and looked up from the carpet where my gaze had burrowed. "Huh?"

Trish took a step closer to me and said, "What do we do now?"

I looked from her to Henry. There was something in his eyes I couldn't read. I was tempted to label it "lust" but how could he feel that way during a time like this? Unless he was sure death was around the corner and he just wanted to feel some measurement of warmth and love for one last time.

My heart began to race.

"I, uh... Inventory."

"Inventory?"

I nodded and stood from the couch. "Yes, we take inventory of *everything*. Food, water, medical supplies, TP, activities."

"Why?"

"I think decision-making will be faster if we know everything at our disposal."

"Makes enough sense," Henry said, nodding.

I swear he was eyeing my frame the way he did whenever he was horny. Was I looking good? How could I be? I'd run here straight from work. I probably looked like someone pushing through a bender.

"*Okay*," Trish said, dragging the word out. "Then what?"

"I could ask if you have an emergency radio down here but I wouldn't have to if we'd done inventory already," I said pointedly.

"Fine. Let's do that."

I held up my phone and said, "I will just type every-thing in here. But, seriously, *do you* have an emergency radio down here?"

Trish looked at her husband, unsure.

"Um…" Henry turned in place, looking around. "We should have one of those weather radios, if you think that might tell us anything."

"I don't see why the government would hold back sending a signal any way they can," I told him.

Henry moved toward the bathroom door. "Let me look around. We either stored it down here or in the upstairs closet."

With that, Trish and I looked toward the ceiling, lis-tening to the man upstairs. He was quiet now. Dead maybe. Then again, I hadn't heard the sound of him collapsing so maybe he was standing someplace. Or he'd gone to the next floor. Or he'd died sitting down on the couch. The problem was, without the security cameras working, we didn't know anything that was happening overhead.

Henry made a bit of noise from the bathroom as he looked through everything on the thin shelving unit they had in there by the sink. Unlike upstairs, the basement bathroom did not include a closet of any kind.

Trish was feeling understandably antsy, and went to the bar to look through the cupboards there, just in case.

A minute later, Henry returned with a respirator mask in hand, but no radio.

"What the hell is that?" I asked.

"It's usually used for painting," Henry said on approach, "but we used it during the pandemic a bit. Do you think it could work upstairs?"

I took the mask from him and looked it over. "Maybe. It's impossible to know if those filaments were accompanied by anything microscopic." I sighed, thinking it over. "Do you have protective goggles?"

He shook his head. "No. What do you think would happen? To exposed eyes, I mean."

I mulled it over. "That shit is building up on trees and things, so...I would guess it could blind you."

"I wonder how fast..."

"Let's keep that idea in the back pocket for now," I said.

Trish left the bar and joined us. "Nothing."

"The radio must be in the upstairs closet," Henry said.

"Well,"—I sighed and rubbed hands over my tired face—"I suppose we just wait and survive for now. And if something changes or we run out of supplies, then we send someone upstairs to check shit out and get the radio or whatever else we may need."

Everyone agreed and shuffled their feet, not sure what to do next.

Henry checked his watch and said, "I know it's not night yet but...I desperately want to close my eyes."

I looked at my sister and saw her emotional exhaustion. Fear can drain a person. I'm surprised more people don't take naps in horror movies, to be honest—I'd be desperately searching for a cupboard to sleep in if some hockey-mask-wearing-motherfucker was hunting down me and all my friends. But I guess the three of us were weird. Because we all wanted to sleep a bit and refresh before coming up with a new plan.

"Let's do it," I said. "Go to bed for a bit. We'll be more alert after and, hopefully, there will be news to help us decide what to do."

Henry and Trish curled up together on the couch with a blanket thrown over them. I turned off the lights and situated myself on the recliner.

In the darkness, Trish said, "What about the guy upstairs?"

I listened to the house for a moment, ears straining hard, before responding. "I don't think he's looking for us or anything. It's too quiet."

"Do you think he's dead?"

"Maybe. He might have gotten too much exposure before breaking in."

Nobody said anything after that. I could hear one of them snoring five minutes later. I did my best to sleep and closed my eyes, though the stillness of the surrounding world at 7 p.m. was deeply unnerving.

A tremor woke us hours later. I half-jumped, half-fell out of the recliner in my surprise. When I looked around and saw nothing in the darkness, I pulled out my phone and used its screen to find the light switch. Trish and Henry both groaned as the basement was illuminated.

I looked at my phone before pocketing it. The time read 3:57 a.m.

"What the hell was that?" Henry asked, groggy, swinging his legs over the side of the couch and rubbing his eyes.

Trish was moving around the perimeter of the room, looking for something. I wasn't sure what.

"Was it an earthquake?" I asked them.

Trish stopped by the vent on the far wall and cursed. "Guys, we're contaminated."

Henry and I hurried over to her and took a look for ourselves. Though the vents were closed, a red film had appeared along the tight grates. I wasn't at all surprised, but upset that the infiltration had come so fast.

"What about the towel under the door?" Henry asked.

I took the stairs two at a time to check. The towel looked as if it was collecting blood from under the door. I nodded to myself, unsurprised, but cursing nonetheless.

I returned to the others and said, "It's in here with us."

"What does this mean?" Henry asked, looking between me and Trish. "Are we going to die?"

"It's not like there's a lot in here, so I think we'll be okay for a while. Though, it is probably collecting inside us now."

Henry's eyes were red as he turned away to curse and pace across the room.

"What now?" Trish mumbled, turning her lips toward my ear.

"I think…it's time for us to consider moving elsewhere."

"Where?"

I looked toward the stairs and bit my bottom lip. "Here's what we'll do: I'll take the mask and go upstairs, look around. Check outside to see the lay of the land. Find the weather radio. And return. From there, we can see if there are any transmissions, and plan accordingly." I looked from Trish to Henry, who was continuing to pace around the room. "Deal?"

Solemn, Henry nodded but wouldn't meet my gaze. Trish found the mask and handed it to me. "Be careful," she said.

"I'll do what I can," I told her with a nervous chuckle.

Once I got the mask secured and my shoes on, I headed up the stairs and paused at the door to prepare myself. I knew my hands were shaking, at the very least. I told Trish to replace the towel once I was through the door, and she nodded at the ready. I then moved the towel out of my way and stepped onto the ground floor, shutting the door behind me as quickly as possible.

On the other side, my eyes began to bother me, itching like an allergy. I ended up putting my hand over them, leaving just a sliver of space to see where I was walking as I looked for the key bowel near the front door. Once I found it, I searched for Henry's sunglasses and put them on. They were not as good as protective goggles, but they were better than nothing.

I got a clear look around myself for the first time. Curls of red were floating in the air around me, as if suspended in a jelly mold. I swiped a gentle, careful hand through the air and cleared a path for myself. It was surreal, though I was sure there were much smaller filaments that continued to evade me—I was only pushing aside the bigger fibers in the path of my face as I moved.

First, I checked the bay window to look outside. The concentration of red curls was incredible. Everything was covered in the stuff, to the point it looked like red snow had fallen across town. Tree limbs were bending under the weight of it, as were electrical wires. The sky was too thick with the red stuff for the stars to show. I wondered if we'd see the sun later or not—there were still a few hours until morning.

As I turned from the bay window to explore the house, I remembered the man who'd broken in. I glanced at the front door and saw that it was shut, but the locks were busted and there were spaces in the frame where the red was seeping inside. The man, however, was nowhere in my vicinity. Assuming he was alive, I wondered if he'd heard me moving around. Surely, he had. I decided to look for him on the ground level before moving upstairs to find the weather radio. Trish thought it might be in the supply closet opposite the bathroom, though she wasn't sure.

The ground level appeared empty. I looked through cabinets and drawers, just in case, but was more interested in finding our squatter. When I had no such luck, I proceeded upstairs—hesitant and swallowing fear in a gulp—with a butcher knife from the kitchen. When I reached the top of the landing and turned into the hallway, I decided to first check Henry and Trish's bedroom. It was undisturbed and almost empty of the red curls. In general, the stuff hadn't traveled upstairs so much yet, which made me wonder how the filaments moved. Were they organic and conscious? Were they pushed down by gravity too much to glide upstairs? I was no scientist and wondered if others would laugh had they heard the questions I posed.

Back into the hallway, I moved toward the office next. It, too, was empty. I thought to check its closet for the radio, and found a toolbox I thought might come in handy in some shape or form, so I put it at the top of the stairs. Then I moved toward the two guest rooms. Trish had always wanted kids, which was why they'd purchased a house of this size. But it had yet to happen, and now it seemed like it never would.

The first room was without a bed, nightstand, or dresser. Instead, it housed bookshelves and labeled boxes of things never unpacked. Perhaps there were seasonal clothes stashed away in some of the totes, but I didn't care. I looked upon them, sadness overwhelming my sense of fear, and figured they would never be opened again.

In the last room, I found the intruders.

There was a young boy, maybe six, tucked into the bed. He was deathly pale and still. Beside him was a washcloth stained with red—I presumed it was blood cleaned by the father, rather than the poison. I thought back to the man outside the house hours earlier. Had he said there'd been an accident? The boy may have died of head trauma at the time. I was sure if I searched his scalp, I'd find a divide. But I had no such curiosity in the matter—seeing the dead child was upsetting enough.

Beside the bed in the rocking chair was the man, bloated around the neck, chest, and underarms as though something large and misshapen was growing inside him. Unlike his son, it was clear the man had died from the poison. Choked on it as it filled his throat and lungs. His nose and eyes were leaking blood, tacky and thick. He was sitting slumped with his hands clasping the arms of the chair in a death grip.

I turned away with tears running down my cheeks. There was this and more, much more, in the houses stretching for miles and miles. It broke my heart, so much so that I considered removing my mask and embracing death right then and there. Instead, I smacked myself hard on the cheek and told myself Trish and Henry needed my help.

I went to the supply closet in the hall and located the weather radio behind a collection of shampoo and conditioner bottles. I then gathered the toolbox from the top step and returned downstairs. At the basement door, I kicked lightly with my foot several times in case they couldn't hear me through the mask. Trish opened the door a moment later and ushered me onto the stairs. As she shut the door behind me, coughing, I found Henry by the bar. I put everything onto the counter and removed the mask, though it looked as if I should keep it on—there were more strings of red floating around the basement, coils of poison we could see and couldn't avoid. It wasn't a lot, but there was still a definitive presence, which suggested there were smaller pieces invisible to the naked eye also swimming up our nostrils as we breathed.

"Shit," I said, looking around. "We need to get moving."

"We only have the one mask," Trish said, coming up from behind me and coughing as she spoke.

"Let's just try the radio before we make any decisions," Henry said, taking the box and cranking it to life with a handle that jutted out of its backend.

"The United States of America is under attack. Please remain indoors, sheltered from the outside." Crackling followed. Then: *"The United States of America is under attack. Please remain indoors, sheltered from the outside."*

"Shit," Trish said, picking up the radio. "Is that all? Is it just going to keep repeating that?"

They waited a full minute before shutting off the radio. In that time, the message played more than twenty times.

Henry grabbed the radio and chucked it across the room. "FUCK!"

I looked at Trish but said nothing. We were all angry.

Leaving the bar and walking back and forth across the basement, Henry finally stopped before us and said, "We need to get reconnected to the internet. Find out what's going on. Somewhere, someone is posting every update they can find."

"How?" I asked.

"I'll go outside and clean the equipment."

"I'll come with you."

"We only have the one mask. You and Trish stay here." He sighed as he looked toward the stairs. "I'll check the neighbors' houses to see if they have any, though. We'll need more to get out of here together." He snatched the mask from the counter and put it on.

I handed over the sunglasses and said, "Be careful."

Henry's hand lingered over mine as he took the sun-glasses, but he said nothing. Instead, there was a look of apology in his eyes. Then he turned to Trish, kissed her on the cheek, and hurried up the stairs with the toolkit I'd found in the office. Trish followed, covering the underside of the door once he was gone. When she returned to me, she was crying.

"We're going to die," she said, collapsing onto the couch. "What are we supposed to do? Where are we supposed to go?"

I sat down beside her and put my arm around her shoulders, hugging her close. "We'll figure something out."

"The fucking roads are blocked, so it's not like we can take a car and drive like hell."

"I know."

"So, we're just going to leave on foot?"

"Probably."

Silence descended for some time. I was almost asleep with her on the couch—I swear, the poison we were breath-ing was contributing to our unusual exhaustion—when she spoke again.

"Remember that creek we used to go to all the time as kids? The one in the woods behind the house?"

I nodded with a smile. "Of course."

"Sometimes, I would go there alone."

"And do what?" I asked.

"Think. Draw." She shrugged. "I gave Alan my first handjob there."

I laughed and pushed my sister from me. "Why would you tell me that?"

She smiled. "To get a reaction out of you," she said. "I was hoping you'd find it funny."

"Alan was my friend! I don't want to think of my sister fucking him."

"I did *not* fuck him. I just got him off the one time."

We were both laughing. It felt good, but it also felt wrong, like we'd forgotten the situation, forgotten Henry, who was out there somewhere risking his life to reconnect us to the rest of the world.

I did my best to push this out of my head as we reminisced. It seemed like we needed it more than we wanted to admit. Laughter was medicine, as were memories. *Good* memories, at least. The other kind were dangerous. Deadly. My mind wandered to darker places as we talked. I tried to push those memories away—push them back into their locked chests in the attic where they belonged—but I was ashamed and hurt to find memories of Henry were now there as well. Dark to me instead of light. Maybe it was my guilty conscious clawing forth at the reality of death approaching.

"When was the last time you talked to any of them?" Trish asked me.

I blinked and tried to remind myself what she'd been saying. "Talk to who?"

"Alan, Bree, or Sean."

"Oh. Um…years. Not since graduation."

"None of them?"

I shrugged. My mind was blank, save for Henry and what we'd done behind my sister's back for most of their marriage. I tried asking about her childhood best friend, but Trish waved a hand between us to cut me off.

"What are we doing?" she asked.

I felt my nerves spasm within me. "What do you mean?"

"All this pretending. All the time. Even before the attack."

"I, uh… I don't follow."

"Yes, you do," she said, looking hard into my eyes. "I know all about it."

"About what?"

I couldn't help but swallow as I tried to control my breathing. I must have looked obvious but I was tired and scared.

Scared of everything in that moment.

The poisoned clouds. The conversation. What the future held, however much was left of it for us.

"You and Henry," she said, leaning back against a pillow. "You've been... What? *Dating* for a while now."

I looked away from her and shut my eyes tight, as if I could wish away the confrontation. "I..."

"You what?"

I took a deep breath and ran my tongue over my teeth. How much time had passed since Henry left? At what point should we have gone looking for him?

"Mark."

I opened my eyes and met her gaze. "What do you want me to tell you?" I asked.

"How long?"

"The first time was two years ago."

"How often?"

"Occasionally. We don't plan for it." I looked down at the floor. "Not often, at least."

"Are you two in love or something?"

"I don't know what Henry feels."

Trish wiped the tears from her face as she sobbed. "I guess we could call ourselves even," she said.

"What do you mean?" I asked, keeping my eyes down.

"I was the one who told Mom and Dad you were gay."

I couldn't help but laugh. I don't know why. It didn't matter that what my sister did destroyed my relationship with our parents. I laughed and so did Trish. But it was over within seconds.

"I'm sorry, Trish," I said, closing my eyes again. "I felt something for him and let impulse take over."

"Do you love him?"

"Maybe. I think so. But I've always…pushed away those feelings because of you." I tried not to but I began coughing.

Trish ignored it and said, "I don't see how I could factor into that equation. I couldn't have been considered much for you to have started fucking him in the first place, could I?"

I cleared my throat and nodded. "I don't know what I can say to make any of this better," I told her. "But I am sorry. I never meant to fall for him. I never looked for a way to hurt you. None of that was ever intended."

She looked away from me and stood. "It doesn't matter anymore," she said, sighing. "Nothing does. We're going to die soon anyway." She left the couch and crossed over to the bar to pour herself a hard drink.

I checked my phone to see the time. It was a little after 4 a.m. and my battery was getting low. I pocketed the device and stood. "How long do we give him out there?" I asked.

Trish poured herself another shot and threw it back. "An hour more."

"Really? That long?"

"If he's dead, he's dead, Mark. There's little we can do about it."

I opened my mouth to say something, but found the words missing. So, I turned away and walked up the stairs to take a seat in a narrow space where there was some sense of undeserved security I couldn't help but cling to. Around the corner, I heard Trish hacking into a rag.

When Henry returned, it was nearly 6 a.m. and the darkness outside was receding. He was wearing safety goggles and had a pack with him that he tossed onto the couch as he joined us in the basement once more.

"What did you find?" I asked, following him.

Henry lowered his mask and looked between me and Trish. "You two don't look so good."

"Thanks for noticing," Trish said, coughing. It had gotten much worse since he left.

Henry's gaze lingered a moment longer on her before he opened the pack and began pulling things out of it. "I've got everyone a mask and goggles. I also found some handheld radios we can use, and roadside flares. I forgot my tool kit outside, but that hardly matters." He sighed heavily before continuing. He sounded out of breath. "Everything is buried in the red shit. I couldn't get the equipment cleaned in any way that would have made a difference because lines are down everywhere. I'm surprised we still have power. I'm sure that will go soon."

"Where did you get all this stuff?" Trish asked.

"The masks and goggles are from that farm on the corner. I raided one of their barns for a while, trying to decide what to take and what to leave. It was hard to just grab this little bit. But I knew I had a good walk back to the house and didn't know what we really needed. I figured we could always go back there if we needed to."

"What about the radios and flares?" I asked, inspecting one of the handhelds for myself.

"Two different cars," Henry said. "The roads are completely blocked with them. People are dead everywhere. In their cars, their homes, outside... It's horrible."

"Did you find anybody alive?" Trish asked. "The Winslows? Amy? Charles?"

Henry looked away from her and shook his head. "Most people tried to leave and probably inhaled too much of it. There were also other break-ins, like we had here. But our guy at least attempted to shut the door behind him. Other places, it looks like fights broke out. Not everybody died from the poison, judging from what I saw."

I cursed under my breath. "You didn't find a *single* fucking person alive?" I asked.

He swallowed and said, "I didn't search the houses like I wanted to. I was worried someone would shoot me down. I mostly looked through windows and checked people's sheds and outdoor shelters."

"So, there could be others out there."

"Sure. And it's not like I went far. Only a half mile, maybe."

"Well, where should we go?"

He looked between us again, thinking. "I don't know. I guess we could just pick a direction and walk. Maybe the road will clear eventually and we can take a car."

I turned to the stairs and adjusted my mask and goggles. "Then let's eat first and pack some supplies."

We all used the bathroom and grabbed water bottles from the pack I'd brought downstairs the previous night. Then we secured our protective gear and headed upstairs to have an early breakfast. The sun would be rising soon. Removing the towel from beneath the door made my heart skip a beat. We were preparing to leave. The act felt like an acceptance of some kind, though I couldn't quite describe it to myself. But I knew we were choosing to embrace the changed world and find a way to adapt. To survive.

When we went about the kitchen to make breakfast, I wondered if the food was even safe to digest. The moment it was exposed to the air outside its container—whether it be a box or can or bag—was it contaminated to a point of danger? Did it even matter anymore? Though it was in small doses, we'd already breathed the stuff for hours now. Maybe having the squiggles in our lungs was worse than having it in our bellies, but who was I to say with any certainty?

Trish cooked a plate of scrambled eggs for her and Henry while I poured myself a simple bowl of cereal and ate it from a corner of the room, huddled close to the walls. This made me feel better about its exposure to the red. My sister and her husband didn't seem to care that they were using the poison as an ingredient in their breakfasts. I could even see strands of red in their egg whites; it looked a bit like blood. I was sickened by the sight and turned away. But not before seeing Henry take a large bite of the stuff with his eyes closed—perhaps that made him feel better about eating it. I figured Trish was too defeated on the inside to care. I worried she might act foolishly outside if she was already showing signs of giving up.

Once we'd finished eating, we changed our clothes and found ourselves boots to wear. I had to wear Henry's things because the quick bag I'd packed after work was still in my car, somewhere up the road from the house. Henry's clothes were, more or less, my size, but his boots were loose. I wondered how long I could walk in them before it became a problem. Just in case, I kept my own shoes inside the pack I would be carrying.

Before leaving, Henry surprised me by retrieving a pistol from a secret place in their bedroom upstairs. When I told him I wasn't aware he even had a gun, Trish smirked and said, "I guess I still have something up on you then." Though it hurt she was measuring knowledge of Henry against us, I understood she was coming from a place of hurt. I couldn't blame her for wanting to feel some level of superiority over me. She knew Henry had a gun all along, but I did not—that meant she was less in the dark than me, which must have felt reassuring to some degree.

Henry looked between us but said nothing. Was he aware of our private discussion while he was away? Perhaps he could sense it having happened.

When we approached the front door to leave, we all hesitated as a unit to cross the threshold outside. Glances were exchanged but there were no words shared. I was the first to remove my phone, however, to check its signal. The others followed suit. We would check them on occasion as we walked, in the hope that something might change during our walk. It seemed like a longshot, but so did everything at this point.

The world was quiet outside, still and unflinching and red. Stepping onto the front lawn and taking a look around felt surreal in a terrifying way. We didn't know this world. It was different now, unpredictable. It was as if we'd stepped out of our normal lives and into an apocalyptic movie where things slipped off-screen from the corner, hiding and waiting for an opportune moment to strike.

Only, I didn't feel any eyes on us. Not a single one.

There were bodies everywhere as we crossed the lawn in the direction of the road. Some were in the cars where they'd hoped to be safe from the red. After a while, the stuff had slipped inside in clumps and choked them in their sleep. Those that had been alive for their suffocation had tried to flee—there were dozens of people collapsed amongst the stopped cars out front Trish's house. All along the road, car doors were ajar from when the vehicles were abandoned. I found that visual almost as haunting as the corpses scattered across the ground. The red encompassing everything didn't help. Though the sun was rising and we could see the world around us now, the sky was far from clear. A thick red haze remained, though perhaps not as heavy as it was falling the night before. Would it clear with time? It had to, didn't it?

"Which way?" Trish asked from beside the ditch.

I tried to ignore the bloated corpse three feet from her. "Left," I said. "Downtown might be good to check."

"Should we go to your car first?" Henry asked, looking right. "You didn't have your bag with you."

"No. I left it in the passenger's seat." I considered the bag's contents a moment before continuing. "Let's leave it. I don't think I brought anything worth the trouble." It was hard to care about much of anything.

"If there's something we need," Trish said, "we can just take it as we go. I don't think theft matters anymore. Not here."

It seemed morbid to steal from the freshly dead—many of which had been our neighbors—but she wasn't wrong. Whatever supplies were along the road appeared up for grabs. I hated myself for thinking it, though, and shook my head like an Etch-A-Sketch.

We turned left onto the roadside and weaved through the vehicles, many of which had crashed into the backs and sides of others while trying to escape. I saw people of all ages dead and bloated. Many of them were purple in the face with reddened eyes. Though I tried not to look closely at them, I did notice their prominent, engorged veins, even up their arms. It must have been an effect of the poison, one I did not wish to analyze for the time being. So, I pushed it to the back of my mind, hopeful I could keep it there, but doubting my own willpower.

The road curved for some time. Various neighborhoods branched off from it, but the grocery stores and fast food restaurants weren't much further—we had three or four miles to go. Assuming we didn't run into any trouble, we'd find someplace to stop and eat before the normal lunch hour.

Every time the road revealed more of itself, we held our breaths and prayed to find some sort of clearing in the traffic. But every time, we were disappointed with more bumper-to-bumper congestion. We'd been walking for about an hour without sight or sound of anyone when I saw someone drag a corpse into their home ahead of us. At first, I thought I'd imagined it, but then it seemed reasonable to assume the corpse was that of a loved one they hoped to bury. Nevertheless, I pointed out the house to the others and we kept tabs on it as we passed. When Trish asked why we didn't stop to ask word from them, Henry said, "Let the poor bastard grieve. If there was good news, I'm sure they'd have let us know."

I wasn't so sure. Not everyone wants to share their secret to survival.

When the road merged with the old highway ahead of us, it sloped downward and gave us sight of the town below. As we took in the view, our hearts sank. The grocery store was blackened and partially collapsed. An explosion looked to have occurred, though it wasn't clear how or why. The surrounding shops and restaurants weren't in the best of shape either—besides being stained red from the clouds, there were broken windows and small fires actively burning. Throughout the adjoining parking lots, corpses were scattered every few feet in the midst of crashed vehicles. It looked like a massacre.

"Jesus Christ," Henry said.

I tried looking beyond the first strip plaza, where the likes of banks and gas stations followed for a stretch. Over the next hill was downtown, which led to the water if you went east.

"Should we look for a boat?" I asked. "Along the bay?"

Trish turned to me and said, "Do you know how to sail?"

"No."

"So, how would a boat be useful to us?"

"It was just a suggestion." I shrugged. "If the roads are fucked, there's always the bay. We could go across and see if the clouds fell everywhere or not."

"It's not a bad idea," Henry said, turning to us. "Town doesn't look any better here, so what's our next move? A boat is at least a plan. Do you have any other?" he asked his wife.

She looked angry to have been asked for a better solution, but said, "I am fine with a boat if someone knows how to work the damn thing."

"I'm sure we can figure it out," I told her. "We get a boat that is, what, automatic? One without the sails and shit, because we obviously don't know how to do any of that. But the ones where the steering wheels and dashboards are like a car... Why not?"

"So, a speed boat?"

"If we can find one."

Henry nodded as he listened. "I say we do it. The houses along the water have their own little piers. We just find a house with a boat we can handle, search for their keys, and get the hell out of here."

"And if the owners are alive?" Trish countered.

"Well, we won't steal from *those* people. Besides, they probably would have left already if they could."

I put my hand on the center of Trish's back to give her a nudge forward. "Let's get moving and just see what we can find. Okay? We still have at least an hour's walk to the water from here. And I don't know about you, but the more we are exposed out here, the less time I think we have to live."

Downtown didn't look any better. Everything we passed was red, on fire, or collapsed. In some places, it looked as if bombs had gone off, leaving behind devastating craters. I thought of the tremors we'd felt overnight and wondered if there had been some sort of carpeted attack. Maybe the poisoned clouds had been part of the first killing wave, followed by a bombing. Were there ground troops sneaking around, too? Cleaning up whoever had survived the night? I shuddered at the thought and kept it to myself. My sister and Henry were anxious enough as it was without me filling their heads with ideas of war, whether civil or foreign.

As we neared the short pier and the neighborhood beside it, we saw the houses were still standing—the tremors might not have reached that far. It was a relief to see only the red, this time. But I also worried this meant we were far more likely to find living opposition while searching for a boat. I didn't want to hurt anyone else's chance to escape. Maybe we could talk someone into letting us join them if we crossed paths with an owner.

All these scenarios flooded my head as we walked in silence. No one had said a word in more than twenty minutes. We were all wrestling with our own thoughts and feelings, most of which were dark and hopeless. It was difficult not to feel lost when the world around you was blanketed in red. The curls drifting around us were akin to spores or ash caught in the breeze—haunting and foreboding. Almost like they represented the calm before the storm. But if it wasn't the storm we'd just experienced, then just what the hell was coming next?

"I need to eat something," Trish groaned as the pier came into full view.

"You think the snack shack is safe?" Henry asked.

"Doubt it," I said, looking in its direction. "I'm sure it's full of the red stuff."

"So, we need a house," Trish said, "to eat safely. Or as safely as we can at this point." She coughed hard and stumbled, a thick drool of red hanging from her lips. Henry caught her but she shook him off. "Have you wondered what it's doing to us?" she asked me. "Do you think it multiplies inside our lungs? Like, even though we only inhaled a little, we're still doomed. These bastards just hit it quicker."

I swallowed. "It's crossed my mind, sure. But if we can get across the water and find somewhere untouched, maybe we can get medical help that—"

"Well we're fucked, Mark," she sneered. "But yeah, let's get a boat anyway. I wouldn't mind some time on the water one last time."

Henry cleared his throat and pointed toward a house on the other end of the playground. "Should we try there?"

"We should break into as few homes as possible," I said. "And that one doesn't have a boat. The houses along the shore down that way do, though. We'll stop at one of them to eat."

Trish loosened her mask enough to slip a cracker into her mouth. When me and Henry shot horrified looks her way, she shrugged and said, "I'm sorry, guys. I… I just don't think I really care anymore."

My heart somehow sank lower. I had worried she'd get like this before anyone else. She was still grieving over the confirmation that her husband had been having an affair with her brother, and that had broken her heart. It was understandable that she'd behave this way, but still terrible to see her give up.

As we walked the rows of houses and watched for signs of life, we realized curtains were fluttering in many of the windows we passed.

"This might not be so easy," Henry said. "Looks like these people may have received enough warning to hunker down."

I cursed. We could always ask to join forces with someone, but it seemed unlikely anyone would open their door for them and risk exposure.

"Can you hotwire a boat without the keys?" Henry asked.

"I have no clue."

"I'll check my phone, see if I can get any connection down here." He slipped out his device and tried Google. When it failed to load any results, he threw the phone through the air in frustration. It shattered upon impact with the road some forty feet from us. "Goddamn it!" he screamed, stopping and swinging his fists through the air like someone in a mosh pit. "Fuck this! Fuck it! Fuck it! Fuck it!"

Trish took a seat in the red-smothered grass and watched her husband, disinterested.

I was beginning to worry more by the second. Both of them were becoming lost causes. I wondered if I should leave them, find a way to safety, and then return to them once I had things set up. But what if I couldn't get anything prepared without having to flee? Then I wouldn't have the ability to get them later.

To my right, a man wearing some sort of cosplay helmet was watching us from the window. I doubted his costume was protecting him but maybe he didn't care. Maybe he was in denial. Maybe I was, too, a little. I wasn't willing to give up like Trish and Henry. I couldn't accept a future that would end this week, if not sooner.

I crossed the yard toward the guy in the helmet and waved at him on approach. When I felt I was close enough to be heard, I called to him through the glass. "Do you have a boat? It might be safe for everyone if we cross the bay."

The man looked over his shoulder. I couldn't tell if he was just considering the idea or talking to someone I couldn't see. A moment later, he turned back to me and pointed down the road.

"*You* don't have a boat?" I clarified.

The man shook his helmeted head.

I gave a weak smile and thanked him. "Let's go," I said to Trish and Henry. "We can't just stop here and wait around for things to change themselves."

"Maybe we can," Henry said, shrugging. "Have you ever seen that movie, *The Mist*? What if we go through hell just to find the military solving all our problems a second later? Sometimes, waiting is enough."

I scoffed. "I'm not convinced the military or government didn't have something to do with all this. So, I'm not going to wait around for them."

Henry looked over at the man in the window with his helmet still hiding his face from us. Though I was no longer speaking with him, the guy had continued to watch us with what I assumed was interest. Maybe not in our wellbeing but in what we tried to survive.

"What are you thinking?" I asked Henry.

He broke his gaze from the helmeted man and turned back to me. "I think I want to wait."

"Here? Outside?" I shook my head. "Can we at least find an empty house?"

"Are you agreeing to wait if we do?"

"I'm agreeing to stay with you long enough to formulate a plan that I may or may not have to do alone if you've decided to stop trying."

Henry didn't reply. Instead, he looked over at his wife, who shrugged. I wouldn't have been surprised if she'd laid back in the red fluff and remained there until the end. Her mind had fractured at some point during our walk through town. Maybe it was all the death we'd seen. Hundreds of corpses, young and old. It's hard to shake that. I'd done my best not to think of it, but I was scared they'd haunt my dreams whenever I next went to sleep. Or maybe I'd never be able to sleep again.

"Let's find someplace," I said, beginning to walk once more down the road. "We can consider our options again once we're situated inside someplace."

To my surprise, Trish stood to follow. She and Henry even went as far as to hold hands as they walked behind me, content to let their problems die before them.

Around the curve, I checked a house that looked eerie and abandoned in its stillness. The yard was unkempt and there were packages on the porch. When I approached the front door, I saw a note taped to the surface above the locks that read PLEASE CALL US, JAY! WE CAN EXPLAIN!

I turned away from the note and cursed under my breath. I couldn't help but wonder if this poor bastard had been betrayed by his spouse and sibling as well. They'd tried to reach him several times before resorting to an uninvited appearance outside his home. If the ignored note, lawn, and packages were any indication, I could guess what awaited us inside.

"What are you doing?" Henry asked me from the yard.

"There was a note. I, uh… I think you guys should just wait out here a minute."

Henry didn't argue.

Trish didn't even acknowledge our conversation. She was looking at the bay beyond the house.

I tried the door and was not surprised to find it locked. I tried knocking and listening, but all was quiet as expected. So I took a stone from the garden's border and used it to break the locks and shouldered the door open. Though I had damaged it, I shut the door as best I could behind me to keep from letting in too much of the red. We could always barricade the door later if we decided to use the house. Maybe go upstairs to stay, seeing as the red coils didn't seem to rise very easily.

The house was dark. I called out to announce myself but nobody answered. I didn't have to go far to find what I wasn't anticipating with dread—a corpse in the kitchen. I assumed this must have been Jay. He was clutching a shotgun in his hands between his legs, and was seated in a dining room chair. His head was mostly gone, fragmented across the kitchen counters and floors. I wasn't surprised but I was still disgusted. I lifted my mask just enough to vomit and wipe my mouth clean before securing it once more.

After a moment of hesitation, I retrieved the shotgun from the man and checked him for ammunition. He hadn't bothered to bring any extra with him, not that I could blame him. Somewhere in the house, there could have been a box of shells. I would have to look for it later. For now, I just needed to confirm the house was empty.

Several minutes later, I opened the front door to usher Henry and Trish inside. Once they were in the foyer, I shut the door and moved a hallway table in front of it. I'd also found a roll of duct tape, which I then used to seal the border of the door better. Neither Mark nor Trish helped me. They were looking toward the open kitchen space where I had tossed a sheet over Jay's corpse. Though his blood still stained many surfaces, his ruined head was at least hidden from them.

"The previous owner," I told them. "Suicide. Probably from a couple days ago."

Henry nodded. Trish remained still.

"Let's stay upstairs," I told them. "This poison doesn't rise very well. I noticed that back at your place."

Though they were silent, they followed me upstairs to the main bedroom. With the door closed, their masks came out, though mine remained. Maybe I was grasping at straws at this point or trying to make a statement, but I didn't want to expose myself if I could avoid it. No one *likes* to wear masks, but if it could save my life, then I'm going to keep it on as much as I can.

"What now?" Henry asked as he took a seat on the bedside with his wife.

I moved to the window that overlooked the bay. I hadn't yet checked behind the house, so I held my breath and took a look below. "Oh, thank god," I said, nearly laughing in relief. "We have a boat."

"The kind we can drive?" Henry asked.

"Yes. There are no sails that I can see."

"So, we just need to find the guy's keys."

"Right."

Trish brought her pack forward and began rummaging through our snacks. "I need to eat before worrying about anything else. I feel incredibly weak." She wheezed as she spoke, a fierce cough echoing through the room.

"You're right," I admitted. "We should get some rest and eat. Use the bathroom if you need to. I have no idea what's on the boat."

"What if someone thinks of the boat before we get a chance to use it?" Henry asked me.

"I'll find the keys now, and get that part out of the way. I don't think anyone will be able to leave with it otherwise."

"Unless it's possible to hotwire a boat," Henry said, mostly to himself, smiling like he was on the inside of a cruel joke.

"Well, let's hope it's not. And if it is, that nobody around here is capable of doing it."

"What about gas?" Trish said.

"Gas?"

"I'm sure the boat uses gasoline or something for fuel, Mark."

I hadn't considered that. "Shit. Well…I'll look for that as well. Even if it has fuel right now, we'll probably need to travel with extra. I'll see if I can find any."

"You do that," Trish said, unwrapping an energy bar and taking a bite.

I looked at them for a moment longer before turning away to search for everything. Though I was also tired and hungry, I wasn't yet ready to rest. I wanted to make sure everything was in place for us to leave first. Then I could take my own break.

The keys on a hook by the back door. As for fuel, there was nothing inside the house, so I headed outside to where there was a small shed by the trees. It was locked, so I had to kick the door open. It wasn't a sturdy shed by any means, so I didn't even hurt myself getting in. Inside, I found some paddles, fishing gear, a lawnmower and other yard tools, gloves, lanterns, batteries, and two large red containers of fuel.

"Jackpot," I said.

I spent the next fifteen minutes loading everything of use onto the boat, including the fishing gear. It hurt that neither Henry nor my sister ever came looking for me, but I told myself to think of them as kids moving forward. I was looking out for their best interests while they ignored my existence. This was practice for parenthood, something I would never experience now that the area was covered in poison red dust.

For the thousandth time, I wondered if the red had blanketed the entire country or just this region. I prayed it was something we could escape, though I knew the world was already forever changed by the event. I was too.

It seemed good that the water wasn't affected by the stuff—whatever coils fell into the bay appeared to dissolve on impact. I wouldn't drink the water or even swim in it if I could avoid it, but I didn't see dead fish floating about either—that gave me hope that it wasn't being poisoned.

When I returned inside to take my own break, I found Henry and Trish in the bed, under the blankets and snuggled together. Their eyes were closed and their breathing shallow. I decided to leave them alone and went into a different room instead to relax. After eating from my pack of snacks, I stretched on the smaller bed and got comfortable.

It took me only minutes to fall asleep. When I woke up hours later, I didn't know how much time had passed but I figured it had to be midafternoon. I glanced in the direction of my window and saw that the sun hadn't set yet. However, it did appear very hazy outside, perhaps even smoky. A pink glow showed across the sky as if somehow amplified by this thickness. It was both beautiful and haunting. The red coils were likely the culprit.

When I opened the door to step into the hallway, I froze at the realization that there were filaments levitating upstairs now by the thousands. Where the hell had they all come from? I hurried downstairs to check the doors and windows and found that someone had removed my blockade in the foyer and opened the front door. When I moved around the back, I found that door was hanging open as well. I rushed over and slammed it shut without looking outside.

"Who would do this?" I demanded the empty room.

When nobody answered me, I shut the front door, moved the table in front of it once more, and hurried upstairs to check on Henry and Trish. As I neared the room, my chest seized at the sight of their door having been left ajar by me earlier. I cursed myself for having fucked up, and burst into the room. Trish was no longer there, but Henry was.

He was dead.

His neck was bloated like a bullfrog and red tendrils were stretching out of his nostrils. Even his chest looked to have expanded outward, full of the mossy shit.

I collapsed to my knees and cried, smacking my palms again and again on the wooden floor.

It took me several minutes to pick myself and clear my head enough to ask the question, just where the fuck was my sister if not here with Henry?

And who had left all the downstairs doors opened?

"No." I said it aloud to help convince myself she hadn't done it herself. "No, no, no."

She'd been lost, but not so far gone as to orchestrate her husband's own death... Right?

I returned downstairs on shaking legs without any of our things. For the moment, I wanted revenge. Maybe Trish had been kidnapped by whoever had infiltrated the house. It made perfect sense—she was a woman and desperate men made monsters. I walked to the front door and threw the table into the foyer wall, leaving behind an angled hole. I then stomped outside onto the porch and took a look out across the street. Nothing caught my eye, other than the sky above— it was much clearer out this way.

Something made my brain itch then, and so I turned. I hurried through the house to the back door and threw it open. As I stepped out into the backyard, I began to scream in disbelief and fury.

The boat was on fire and sinking. The gasoline containers were in the grass, one on its side and empty. The other still contained fuel but it no longer mattered.

A crushing weight of hopelessness brought me to my knees for the second time in minutes.

Trish was sitting on the pier's edge, kicking her legs out over the water with a horrendous cough. When she turned her head to look my way, I saw there was fuzzy mush growing out of her ears and nose. Her eyes were also red from blown blood vessels and contamination. When she opened her mouth to usher me over—"Mark, over here"—I saw her tongue had swollen and her neck was engorged. Though I somehow understood what she said, the words were muffled.

"What have you done?" I asked her on approach. "How could you fucking do this to us?"

"It's time," she told me. "Whether this stuff is man-made, natural, or alien. It's our sign that our end has come."

"You're delirious, Trish. Upset. Losing it! We don't even know how widespread this is. We need to leave."

Trish shook her head with a sad smile. She looked vile and misshapen. How much longer did she have? Her mind was already going or gone. That was clear. She'd killed her husband faster and destroyed our escape. Now I needed to figure out something else alone, because I doubted she would be coming. This was goodbye.

I started approaching her for a hug, but thought better of it. I stopped several feet from her and watched her close. I could see her eyes twitching every few seconds, and when she moved any part of her body, she winced.

"Does it hurt?" I asked her.

She nodded, eyes brimming with sadness and regret.

"Wait here," I told her, turning back to the house and heading inside. I located the shotgun, checked its chamber for a shell, and returned outside with fresh tears on my cheek. When Trish saw me coming, she nodded and shut her eyes.

"I love you, Mark," she said. "I'm sorry."

"I love you, too," I cried as I raised the shotgun and pressed it against the back of her head. Before pulling the trigger, I shut my eyes as well. The shot was loud, despite the muffling of Trish's hair, and powerful enough to push me back several steps. I heard the splash of Trish's body a moment later as it toppled into the water. I refused to open my eyes, though. Not so quick.

My ears rang as my hands shook with the aftershock of the blast. I counted to sixty before leaving the pier. As I neared the house, the boat erupted as the fire burned into its fuel tank, sending pieces of the boat into the air. As the debris rained down around the yard and water, I looked back and wondered what to do next.

I was all alone.

While repacking—taking this and that from the other packs and the house—I grieved. Returning to the master bedroom was difficult for me but I did my best not to look at Henry's body again. I found what I needed and hurried out of there.

Once I had my pack ready to go, I headed downstairs into the kitchen and ate an early dinner. It was getting too late to try finding another house and boat, so I decided I would sleep downstairs. Though the house was full of red filaments, I still had my mask and goggles to protect me. I knew they weren't at all foolproof, but I was having trouble caring. It seemed improbable I would get very far on my own. And would it really matter if I found someplace free of the red? I tried telling myself I still had plenty to live for, but I couldn't help but also wallow in my losses.

There were so many dead around me. It looked like the world had shut off. Why should I push on?

After eating, I made myself comfortable on the couch and tried the TV. Though this street still had power, there was nothing being broadcasted. Some sort of blackout was in effect. The same could be said about cell phone signals. Anything that could connect us to others was unresponsive. When I tried the weather radio, it was no longer playing the message it had before. Now, there was only silence.

In the morning, I left the house and stepped into the street. Maybe I'd find a boat. Maybe I wouldn't. I had lost my sense of urgency to fight forward. What would come would come.

I couldn't save them. Should I bother saving myself?

I took a deep breath and began to walk.

The sky was turning red again.

SPECTRUM

Barry thought he was going to change his life for the better, taking Arlene to Las Vegas and surprising her with an engagement ring. Instead, he led them into an unexpected change. They were on a stretch of I-15 with little to see but desert and distant mountains when Arlene proposed a game in which they painted their perfect futures to one another.

"A Colorado cabin," Arlene said with a contented sigh and brimming smile. "Up in the mountains with snow and nothing but a small town or ski resort nearby."

"That does sound nice," Barry admitted. "I don't care much for neighbors, you know."

Arlene patted him on the knee as he drove and said, "I know you don't."

"Imagine the pictures I could take." Barry was an amateur photographer with an expensive Canon camera. He loved the snow and wilderness aesthetic but had been born and raised in central California. "Hell, I might even take up bird watching."

"I would love some feeders outside in the yard. Maybe some elaborate birdhouses."

Barry grinned. "Shoot. This future does sound nice."

Arlene squeezed his knee this time and asked what he'd like, assuming her Colorado cabin wasn't good enough for him. Barry laughed and said, "No, no. You painted a wonderful picture. I'm right there with you."

"What about kids?" she asked.

"What about them?" He was only playing dumb—they'd discussed kids on their third date to make sure they were on the same page. Arlene wanted two or three. Barry had told her was open to having "little clones" to help him form a punk band someday.

"You know what I'm asking you," Arlene said, taking her bottled water from the cupholder. It was damn hot outside.

"I'll put a kid in you whenever you're ready." He joked. "You just tell me when and where."

"What if I said 'right here, right now?'"

With no one else on the road with them, Barry swung his car onto the roadside and hit the brakes. Arlene braced herself and laughed, spraying the dash with water.

"You might want some sunscreen," Barry told her, unbuckling his seatbelt. "The sun's mighty strong."

Arlene gave him a playful smack and said, "Jesus, Barry! I was only kidding."

They were about to pull back onto the road when something winked at them a hundred yards away, like a reflection of sun off a mirrored surface. Barry paused with his seatbelt in hand across his chest, not yet secured in its lock. "What's that, you think?"

Arlene leaned forward and squinted through her sunglasses. "Is it in the center of the road?"

"Sure looks like it."

Arlene looked over her shoulder between their seats and said, "Well, this guy can find out for us."

A minivan was approaching from their rear, moving fast. As they zipped past Barry's Camry a moment later, Arlene caught a glimpse of three kids and their parents. The winking light was just ahead of them, but the minivan made no move to avoid it. When the two collided, there was a burst of colored light that blinded both Arlene and Barry. They turned away in unison and cursed. When they looked back, the minivan was nowhere to be seen. The stretch of I-15 ahead of them was clear, with the exception of the small, winking light.

"Did... Did they just disappear?" Arlene asked, flabbergasted.

Barry nodded, then opened his door and stepped out into the road without first checking for others coming from behind him. They were alone once more—the minivan was, indeed, missing. Barry looked back at Arlene and said, "Did we imagine them? Some sort of...collective heatstroke mirage?"

Arlene got out of the car and joined him in the road. "Not a chance. What do we do now?" She looked behind them and saw no one else approaching in either direction. "Should we wait around and see if it happens again?"

"There were kids in there," Barry reminded her. "If they're in trouble, shouldn't we try to help? We can't just sit here and wait around for someone else to get hurt."

"How are we supposed to help? They just vanished into thin air!"

"Maybe... Maybe we saw a ghost," Barry suggested, nodding to himself. "Yeah. Maybe that was a family that died on this highway some time ago and we just saw some of their final moments in a ghostly, uh, time lapse or whatever."

Arlene swallowed hard and looked around them to make sure nothing or no one was sneaking up on them. "Can we leave?" she asked, shaken and wrapping her arms around herself. "Whether they were ghosts or sucked into the void, I don't want to be here any longer."

Barry looked from her to the twinkling ahead. "Stay with the car," he told her. "I'm going to take a closer look at that reflected light. Just so we can rule out what happened."

Arlene opened her mouth to argue, but stayed with the car, nervous and unsettled. She watched Barry walk along the roadside for a hundred or so feet before stepping into the middle of I-15 without a car in sight. He was nearing the source of the blinding flash now. She watched as he looked back at her and reached into his pocket.

What's he doing? she wondered.

He was holding something up now. His phone maybe?

Arlene's cell began to ring from the cupholder. She answered it and heard Barry on the other end. "Hey," he said.

"Hey. So, what is it?"

"It's really strange."

"That's not very helpful." She watched as Barry seemed to circle the light in the distance. "What the hell are you doing?"

"Babe, it's, uh… It's just a floating hole of light and color. I couldn't tell that from the car, but it's beautiful. It's like a tiny, levitating rainbow, the full arch. And it seems to, uh, follow me whichever way I look at it, no matter where I stand. Like one of those creepy paintings with the eyes that are always watching you."

"Well, get away from it and let's go."

"But…we haven't figured out what happened to the van. Hold on. I've got an idea."

She watched as Barry moved toward the roadside, dragged his foot around the ground in search of something, and then bent down to pick up a discarded water bottle. He held it up for her to see and said into the phone, "Let's see what happens when something touches it." He moved back into I-15 and toward the light. He then lobbed the bottle into the blinding hole, making it vanish. "I'll be fucked in the ass," Barry said, excitement lacing each word. "Babe, this is like… I don't know. A portal or some shit!"

"What do we do?"

Barry began walking back toward her, away from the light. "Should we call the police? I don't know how to call the CIA," he said with a laugh.

"What about that family?"

Barry paused mid step before continuing. "Shit. I don't know."

"Let's just call someone. They can figure it out."

Barry was close enough that he was able to end the call and slip his phone back into his pocket. As he neared the car, Arlene jumped up and embraced him. She was shaking and desperate to leave.

"I don't think we can go if we're going to get the police here," Barry told her. "For one, they'd probably just drive through it like that van. We need to try to keep people from touching it."

It took Arlene several minutes to relax, but in the end she agreed. "Only if I can stay in the car."

"Deal. Let's park across both lanes to stop cars from coming."

"The other side of the light would still be exposed," she said.

"Damn. I don't know what to do about that. I guess we can park the car one way, and then I'll stand in front of it from the other way to redirect traffic around it."

"Good thing there's nothing out here." Arlene sighed, looking down the long stretch of highway.

"Small mercies, yeah?"

By the time the police arrived, Barry had only handled three cars on the highway, none of which gave him worse than "What the fuck are you doing in the middle of the road?"

A squad car pulled up to them twenty minutes later, with two officers inside. They came from the direction with Barry's Camry blocking the road. When they stepped out into the blazing sun, they approached Barry at the same time at the same speed, as if in perfect sync. Their name tags read SIMMONS and CLAYTON. Simmons was short and solid, with a shaved head. Clayton was tall with a sharp chin and long, spider-like fingers that rested on his belt.

"Afternoon," Simmons said as they neared. "We received a call about a sinkhole in the middle of the road?" The officer looked beyond Barry and spotted Arlene in the Camry behind him.

The sinkhole was the best they could come up with on the phone. There was no way Barry could tell the dispatch officer people were vanishing into an inexplicable spectrum.

"It's actually a little worse than a sinkhole," Barry admitted to them.

"How so?" Clayton asked, studying Barry.

"It's behind my car," Barry said, turning to show them.

"No, you stay right here," Clayton told him.

Barry paused and straightened. "Okay," he said. "But don't touch it. A minivan with a family inside vanished when they drove through it."

Simmons and Clayton exchanged a look before giving Barry's Camry a wide berth and moving to the other side. Though Barry remained in place, he turned around to watch them. Within seconds, the officers came back around to him and mumbled, "I'm going to be straight with you, sir." He cleared his throat. "We're not with the police."

Barry's chest seized in warning.

"You see, when you took out your phone to call your wife from beside this anomaly, certain agencies were able to

167

view your surroundings. What you found was immediately documented. Gears began turning. Things were prepared."

Barry was confused, but also thought he had some idea where this was headed. "Are you CIA?"

The officers (or agents) exchanged a look before Simmons replied, "Something like that. We were sent here to confirm the finding. There are others converging on this location as we speak. Traffic has been stopped five miles from here in both directions to make sure nobody comes through."

Barry's natural instinct was to look both ways down the road. It was quiet and empty. "What happens now?" he asked.

"A quarantine of sorts. But you won't have to worry about that," Clayton explained, taking Barry gently by the arm and directing him around the Camry, toward the levitating spectrum. "We have this handled."

"What is it?" Barry asked as they stopped in front of the colorful light.

"That's what we intend to find out."

"Will my wife and I have to go into WITSEC or anything for finding this? Or sign an NDA or something?"

Clayton shook his head. He towered over Barry—not that his height was menacing considering his gangly frame, but his eyes were cold and calculating. Before Barry could react to the warning he felt from looking into them, the agent shoved him forward into the spectrum.

Arlene screamed from inside the car, but Simmons was already there, blocking her escape. Barry had vanished like the minivan, and it was the police officer that had done it to him. The vulture-like one was now turning back to the Camry and staring hard at her through the passenger window.

She had nowhere to go but into their arms. She tried to run and fight them, but it was no use. Clayton held under the arms and around the chest while Simmons secured her legs together. The officers then carried her to the colorful light and tossed her inside. Her screams vanished in an instant.

With the couple taken care of, Simmons called in Phase 2. He then put the Camry into neutral, disengaged the E-brake, and he and Clayton pushed it into the spectrum. Though it was being devoured inch by inch as it moved through the light, there was no sound, no crunching metal or exploding fluids. The vehicle simply smeared at the edges as it was swallowed by the spectrum and taken elsewhere.

Once the vehicle was gone and they were alone on I-15, Simmons shook his head and cursed.

"What is it?" Clayton asked him.

"I hate doing this."

"No one likes it," Clayton lied.

Simmons could see right through him, but he pretended to believe his murderous partner. "How many is that now?" he asked.

"The gateways? This is the seventh for June."

"Jesus. What are they planning to do about it?"

Clayton shrugged and returned to their fake squad car. "That doesn't concern our job," he said, gesturing for Simmons to pick up the pace. "Let's go. Phase 2 is closing in. We have other places to be, other things to do."

Simmons looked back at the spectrum one last time before taking a deep breath and getting into the car with Clayton. As they turned themselves around to go back the way they came, helicopters appeared overhead with equipment hanging from wires beneath them.

BURNING DAWN

"**I** hate this job."

Stephen Faris took several deep breaths in an attempt to steel himself, but it was no use. How could one prepare for infiltrating a Tyrannosaurus nest? Even armed, it seemed like a suicide mission. Perhaps if he'd been greenlit to use explosives, he'd feel better. But his rifle—as large and powerful as it was—held tranquilizers instead of bullets. He knew the reaction was instant upon implantation in the Rex's scaly skin, but there was something bothersome about putting his life on the line with the function of a loaded dart. Maybe it was because he'd never trusted one before. Or maybe it wouldn't

171

matter what his rifle fired because, either way, he was facing down a damn dinosaur.

"*Faris. Update.*"

Stephen pressed down on his earpiece and said, "I'm here."

"*And?*"

Stephen swallowed and propped his head out of hiding for another look below. In the crater, the nest seemed unguarded. Quiet. There were three eggs, none of which had hatched. Yet. Behind Stephen was a hover-cart for transportation. It was pre-programmed for auto-delivery of the eggs to the compound—all Stephen had to do was load its cargo and press SEND on the device panel or his wristwatch. Either way, he was unnecessary to the delivery once the eggs had boarded and the command entered. There was no risk of him dropping the eggs or being derailed by the mother T-Rex during his escape. He could die, but the transport would go on without him. And that's all that mattered to his employers.

"Why was I sent alone to do this shit?" he growled into his earpiece.

"*Matthews got sick. You originally had a partner.*"

"How comforting. And, and how *convenient* for Matthews."

"*Relax, Faris. You have the tranquilizer. Those specialized darts will bring down any dinosaur within a second of impact.*"

"Have they been tested?"

"*Of course. You're not the first soldier to be sent outside the compound.*"

Stephen closed his eyes and tried deep breathing once more. The nest was still quiet and unguarded. If he was going to steal those eggs, he needed to get moving before the parents returned. "Why are these eggs so damn important?" he asked the handler.

"*Cancer research has taken enormous leaps forward with embryonic materials found in these eggs. The T-Rex is not our only specimen—just the hardest to collect.*"

"The damn government already has cures for cancer!" Stephen growled into his earpiece, sweat building over his brow. "Just get them to release the shit."

"*You know they'll never do that.*"

"And what makes you think they won't stop you from doing the same?"

There was silence from his handler for a long moment. Then: "*Get moving, Faris. You're burning dawn. The mother will be back soon.*"

Since the public discovery of Rising Island thirteen months earlier, governments from around the globe had set up stakes along the beaches, erecting a variety of compounds for scientific research and development. Stephen was employed by Heinrich & Bastille, the leading team in behavioral studies of the dinosaurs roaming the island. According to them, it had been learned that the Tyrannosaurus hunts alone in the early morning as the sun is first rising. Later in the day, they hunted in a pack. Unlike in movies, their eyesight was not based on movement. They could see just as well as eagles and were even equipped with stereoscopic vision for hunting in the dark. Though none of this made Stephen feel any better, he understood why it was better for him to infiltrate the nest now as opposed to later.

"Proximity sensors show you're clear…"

As if he trusted those security walls. Trees were always being knocked over or damaged by the movement of these enormous beasts—the company sensors malfunctioned almost hourly and were of little comfort. But Stephen had a secret companion in his left jacket pocket to calm his nerves and give him strength—a bottle of whiskey. As he stood from hiding, he removed the bottle and took a heavy swig.

The nest awaited him.

Stephen began down the crater as carefully as he could manage but there was no clear path. He kept the rifle slung over his shoulder and neck to keep it in place as he slipped and slid his way down to the clearing below. Once he'd reached the bottom, he paused to listen to the surrounding forest. He heard nothing but distant birds and insects.

The eggs were maybe a foot and a half long, he surmised on approach. The cart had a soft basket prepared that could hold two specimens of this size. Stephen had been tasked with the recovery of one, but more if possible. He scanned the crater and reminded himself there was no easy way out—he'd have to climb to some degree one way or another. Had Matthews not been "sick", he could have had a rope system in place to make it easier and faster. But on his own and ill-equipped, Stephen would have to use the sling during his escape. Only one egg could nestle against his chest at a time, so there'd be two trips to make, assuming the mother didn't return too soon.

"I'm getting set to carry the first egg out," he whispered into his earpiece as he positioned the sling with his free hand.

"*Keep it steady.*"

Stephens rolled his eyes and grunted with annoyance.

It wasn't easy positioning an egg of that size and weight into a sling strapped to his chest, especially with a large rifle against his back. He bent his knees in the nest to avoid drops of any height. Twice, he fumbled the egg and almost damaged the shell against the floor of the nest. He took a moment to relax—with another swig of whiskey—before trying a third time. Then, he secured the egg in the wrap and inched up from the nest. By the time he was beginning his climb out of the crater, his back was already aching from the weight strapped across his body. A day of massage therapy would have to follow this mission.

Assuming he survived.

"*You've got company.*"

Of course I fucking do, he thought, searching his immediate surroundings for cover.

"*Move quicker.*"

"Shut up, shut up, shut up," he growled in panic, removing the egg from its sling and placing it in the angled brush. He then removed his rifle and lowered his backside against the incline, sinking himself into the foliage beside the egg. As quietly as he could manage, he readied the tranquilizer to be fired. He had an additional five shots in his utility belt in case they were needed. Though he'd been assured one was enough for a Tyrannosaurus, there was always the possibility more than one dinosaur would rear its ugly head during his recovery of the eggs.

The ground trembled with the approach of something large. Something moving with…a limp?

Stephen clicked on his earpiece. "What's coming?"

"*It's not the mother.*"

"So, what is it?"

From the opposite lip of the crater, a wounded Triceratops appeared. Its horns were red with blood, as was its sheared face. Before Stephen could question its intent, he realized its eyelids drooped, almost shut. The lizard stumbled at the lip, unaware of the drop, and tumbled into the crater a second later with a terrified, animalistic squeal. It landed just shy of the two remaining eggs of the nest, where it remained, listless and shuffling on its side with a pained mewl.

"Shit."

"*Is there a problem, Faris? We can see you have a new friend in your vicinity.*"

"It's dying," he said without clarification.

"*What is? Wait… Faris, you need to hide.*"

Stephen's heart leapt into his throat. "What is it?"

He could hear quickened movement from the direction the Triceratops had come.

"*The sensors are all red.*"

"Meaning?"

"*Hide.*"

The approach sounded like thunder from beyond the crater's lip. Stephen shuffled himself as much into the foliage as he could manage and scooped leaves over his body without restricting his ability to use the rifle if necessary.

Two enormous dinosaurs appeared atop the lip a second later and eyed the dying Triceratops below. They were at least fifteen feet tall and long, with a similar build to a Tyrannosaurus. However, their faces were longer, jaws thinner, eyes smaller. They had the face of a pissed-off reptilian goose, as far as Stephen was concerned.

"*If you can safely do so, send us a picture.*"

Stephen swallowed hard and damned his earpiece. He doubted any dinosaur could hear his handler's voice but didn't know for sure. Slowly, he removed his left hand from the rifle and turned the face of his wristwatch toward the dinosaurs as they began their descent into the crater.

"Record," he whispered into the watch, bringing it closer to his lips for a second.

A red light appeared from its side. Stephen almost cursed aloud, having forgotten the indicator. Luckily, the dinosaurs took no notice of him or the light—they were dialed in on the Triceratops below. As they reached the bottom of the decline and began toward their prey, Stephen filmed a twenty second video before transmitting the file to the compound with a quiet voice command. He then returned his hand to the rifle and steadied his breathing.

"*Keep out of sight, Faris. Those appear to be Carcharodontosaurus.*"

Stephen squeezed his eyes shut in frustration. *As if I know what the hell that is,* he thought.

"*They're bad news. Wait for them to leave.*"

And how long could that take? They were feeding on a fresh kill forty feet away from him. His scent shouldn't be carried in the breeze from within the crater, but they could still take notice of him before long. All it would take would be a simple slip of his boot or—

The egg titled against the brush beside him.

Stephen turned his head to glare at the specimen in warning.

Don't you fucking do it, he thought.

178

The vine nestled at its base bent a centimeter lower, rotating ever so slightly against the weight of the egg.

No. NO.

Stephen removed his left hand from the rifle once more, this time to grab at the egg. But he was too late. The egg began to roll down the decline before he could reel it in towards his body. Though it did not break, it bounced back into the clearing and came to a stop a foot from the crater's curving walls.

One of the Carcharodontosaurus looked in its direction as the other continued its feast of the Triceratops. Curious, it cocked its head and waited for a beat. Stephen clenched his eyes shut and tried not to breathe. The dinosaur took notice of the nest now and approached the two eggs that were closest to it. Stephen opened his eyes to see if he'd been spotted. Instead of a Carcharodontosaurus approaching, he saw the enormous creature using its snout to puncture a Tyrannosaurus egg and eat from it.

Now what was he to do? None of the eggs were with him and he was a sitting duck. The eggs were going to be destroyed soon enough or the mother would return to the nest and protect it from further harm. Either way, it didn't look like he'd be going home with a specimen anymore.

Mission failure.

Stephen was about to press his earpiece and request permission to return to base when the ground began to tremble once more from outside the crater.

I can't believe I'm going to be trapped in a Dino ring of death while Matthews watches TV in his fucking cabin.

Both theropods raised their heads and looked beyond Stephen.

Of course she's returning from behind me, he thought with a contained sigh.

A moment later, the Tyrannosaurus roared from atop the ridge above him, its call ear-piercing. Stephen didn't bother craning his neck to observe its quick descent, but instead prayed he wasn't hiding within its pathway. The crater shook as the mother came crashing down the slope, knocking aside trees with the flick of its thick neck. By a mere foot, it missed crushing Stephen's legs as it passed overhead to charge the nearest Carcharodontosaurus feeding on the egg. Its partner looked up from the gore of the Triceratops and screeched in reply. The Carcharodontosaurus standing over the eggs reared back in preparation for the fight to come.

Stephen took this distraction to roll over and get to his feet. As he climbed up the crater's walls with his body as low as he could manage, the dinosaurs launched into one another below. The ground shook with their collisions, so much so that Stephen lost his footing and slipped more than once. By the time he'd reached the lip and climbed over to where his hover-cart remained in wait, one of the Carcharodontosaurus was bleeding from its neck atop the nest. Beneath it, two of the eggs had been crushed. Only one remained, the egg Stephen had lost along the crater's side wall. It was forgotten as its mother and the remaining Carcharodontosaurus continued their bloody collisions, snapping their jaws against shoulders and sides.

"Shit."

He could still get it, couldn't he? These beasts weren't paying him any mind.

Don't be ridiculous, he told himself. To return to the nest during the fight was still suicidal and stupid.

His handler suddenly sounded from within his ear: "*Do you have the specimens, Faris? I see you've left the nest.*"

Stephen peered into the crater and watched as the two apex predators did their best to kill one another. "Two were crushed," he explained to his handler. "And the other is, uh... pretty close to a battle."

"*What's happening?*"

"The mother returned."

"*Where's the third egg?*"

"Along the side of the clearing."

"*Hold your position, Faris. I'm getting a clearance.*"

A clearance? For what?

As he waited for an answer, Stephen rested his rifle against the tree beside him and took a knee beside the hover-cart to make sure it had remained undamaged by the mother.

"*Faris.*"

"Yeah?"

"*I have received clearance to reward you double for retrieving that remaining egg.*"

Stephen paused. "Did you say double?"

"*That's right. And you'll keep Matthews's original take, as well.*"

Stephen did the math. Bringing home the egg would grant him a payday of sixteen thousand dollars.

He did his best to suppress a smile. "Uh, I'll sure as hell try."

"*Let us know when the egg has been secured in your transport.*"

Stephen returned to the lip of the crater and looked below. Then he collected his rifle and took aim at the Tyrannosaurus. She had to be the priority. And he had an additional five darts. From above the nest, he could safely subdue both predators and return for the egg. He tried lining up his shot along the neck of the mother, but her movements were too frequent. He wondered if the dart would act any less if shot elsewhere. The beast's backside was an easier target, so he shifted his aim and squeezed the trigger. At the same moment, the Tyrannosaurus spun forty degrees with the neck of the

Carcharodontosaurus secured in its jaws. The dart pierced the losing dinosaur's eye, blinding it. The Carcharodontosaurus grunted as its legs gave out beneath it and the Tyrannosaurus released its grip. The Carcharodontosaurus collapsed onto its side and wheezed heavy breaths at its opponent's feet.

Stephen cursed and worked his utility belt for another dart.

The Tyrannosaurus turned its gaze on him.

"Shit!"

He fumbled with a dart and dropped it in the warm soil beneath his boots.

The mother left the side of the dying Carcharodontosaurus and began toward the curving walls.

Stephen collected the fallen dart and tried rubbing it fast against his jacket to clean it of dirt. By the time it was loaded, and he was raising his rifle once more to take aim, the mother was closing in on his location at the lip. He took a step back and stumbled on a root. His shot went awry, and the dart disappeared just above the mother's shoulder. Stephen fell onto his backside and scooted away from the edge of the crater as the Tyrannosaurus emerged.

"Fuckin' hell!"

Rather than load his rifle again with the mother towering over him, Stephen rolled over, scrambled to his feet, and began to run.

"What's happening, Faris?"

The Tyrannosaurus emitted a frightening bellow and gave chase. Stephen weaved in and out of trees in hopes it would slow the mother down, but she crashed through them with ease. He wondered if he could even lose her or if she'd just sniff him out. Maybe if he circled back to the nest, he could still recover the egg. But first, he needed to load his rifle and actually land a dart in the mother. He looked over his shoulder to judge their distance apart and saw that they were abound two hundred yards apart. If he went into the open, she'd surely close that distance in seconds. He knew the Tyrannosaurus could run upwards of seventeen miles per hour, whereas he could only go about seven with the weight of his gear.

Before he could reach the clearing, he turned and began to ark back in the direction of the nest. The mother seemed to pause and reconsider her chase. Taking this as a chance to slow down enough to reload his rifle, Stephen stopped long enough to recover another dart from his belt before running once more. He was already exhausted and gasping for breath, but he couldn't allow himself to be caught.

By the time he was returning to the crater, his vision was doubling, and his head was spinning. He no longer knew where the mother was because his hearing accounted for little more than a heavy pulsing in his ears. As he approached the edge of the crater and looked below, his equilibrium padded forward, and he lost his balance. Stephen tumbled down the crater wall and rolled to the nest below. He landed six feet from the remaining egg with a thud. When he tried to collect himself from the dirt, he screamed in agony—his left arm was broken. Rolling onto his side, pain shooting through him, he scanned his surroundings for his fallen rifle. It took him a moment, but he spotted it part of the way up the incline, tangled in the bushes.

"You've...got to be...kidding me..."

Head still spinning, Stephen sat up in the dirt and began scooting himself toward the egg with his good arm acting as a hook. His legs were bruised and weak. His whole body seemed to be trembling with exhaustion or adrenaline, a mixture that left him feeling more than a little high and unfocused.

"Faris...are...there...you...Faris...respond..."

The pounding in his ears was lessening but he could not yet make out his handler's requests, nor was he interested in hearing them. He had the egg back in hand, but how was he to load it in the sling with a bum arm? Maybe if he rolled up against the incline, he could get it to move backwards into the swaddle on its own. As he made this attempt, the ground shook with the approach of the mother above.

"Of course," he grumbled, doing his best to focus on the egg instead. If he could get it on his person before she neared, maybe the Tyrannosaurus would leave him alone in fear of hurting its unborn young.

"Leverage," he thought aloud. "I need the leverage."

The mother began down the slope toward him with a roar from its enormous jaws, its foot crushing the rifle into the brush along the way. As she moved upon him, Stephen collected the egg in his swath and stood fast to show himself to the Tyrannosaurus, stumbling backwards in the process. As his equilibrium tilted and he fell onto his backside, he pulled back the dark cover enough to expose the side of the egg to its mother as she closed the remaining distance between them.

"Look!" he shouted. "LOOK!"

The beast paused over him, its teeth hovering several feet above Stephen's own. Its breath was hot and putrid. Stephen remained still, terrified. The Tyrannosaurus tilted its nose to the egg and sniffed twice. Then it backed away from Stephen and raised its head to look at him from a vantage point.

Stephen struggled to his feet, careful not to turn his back on the beast at any point. He kept the egg facing its mother and revealed its shell once more once he was steady on his feet. "You hurt me, you hurt this," he mumbled.

The mother stared at him as she shifted her feet every few seconds in impatience.

Now what?

Stephen tapped his earpiece and said, "What are the chances of the mother following me back to the compound?"

"You haven't shot her yet?"

"My gun has been broken."

"Jesus, Faris."

Stephen continued to stare right back at the Tyranno-saurus as she watched him intently. He was too scared to break their connection in fear it would give him away as weaker than he wanted to appear.

"Will you answer my question or not?" he asked.

"*Studies have shown the parents to sometimes starve themselves to protect their nest from scavengers. So, yes, it is possible she will follow you here.*"

"And if she does?"

There was a long moment of silence in which Stephen wondered about signal interference. Then, "*We will disable her and harvest her. An even larger payday for you, assuming things go smoothly.*"

Stephen took in a shuddering breath and said, "Be ready then."

He began to move backward with the Tyrannosaurus glare upon him. Every five feet or so, she would take a step forward, keeping him within snatching distance.

Damn, he thought. *Can I risk turning or not?*

Just as he was about to look over his shoulder, the back of his boot fell upon the nose of the tranquilized Carcharo-dontosaurus. He almost fell in surprise and was horrified to see the Tyrannosaurus had shifted angles in preparation.

She was waiting for him to make one wrong move.

"Damn you," he grumbled, breathless. How was he to climb out of the crater moving backward like this with a broken arm?

The mother's eyes flicked off him. She was now looking beyond Stephen.

What?

He looked behind him and up the ridge. Three camouflaged men were positioned with weapons, one of which was a net gun. They were not from Stephen's company, of that much he was sure.

They were competition.

"Fuck."

The net gun fired, ensnaring the mother's head and miniature arms. She reared back and tried to scream, but her jaw was clamped shut. Stephen remained in place, unsure of where to go. These men would capture him, maybe even kill him depending on their company. As he considered his options, however few, the Tyrannosaurus ducked her head low and dragged it across the clearing to tear the netting.

"You need to leave, Faris."

Stephen snapped out of his daze and ran at a twenty-degree angle around the thrashing dinosaur toward the slope leading back to his hover-cart. Behind him, the men began shouting in a foreign language he could not follow. A rifle fired just as Stephen was reaching the incline and slipped—the bullet pierced the ground beside his hand where it fell.

Stephen cursed and looked back. The Tyrannosaurus scraped her head against the horns of the deceased Triceratops and freed herself. The attention of the armed men on the ridge returned to her instead of Stephen. He thanked the gods and returned to his painful one-handed climb out of the crater as gunfire erupted around the nest. The Tyrannosaurus roared and charged up the ridge toward the men as they scattered, shouting back and forth.

As Stephen crested the slope and leaned against a tree to catch his breath, he looked back at the fight on the opposite end of the crater. The mother was out of the pit now, swinging her angry jaws open and giving chase. One of the soldiers fell and she hurried upon him. Her head snapped forward like a striking snake and removed the man's arm as he unleashed a horrible scream.

Stephen turned away and prepared himself to load the hover-cart with the egg in his sling. As he fumbled to get the egg out of its swath, another gunshot sounded, this time closer. The cart suddenly dipped to the forest floor with a screech and sparks.

"Damn it," Stephen growled, taking refuge behind a tree and securing the egg against his chest once more. One of the soldiers was making his way around the crater toward him. Stephen considered his options. There was still a soldier unaccounted for, being hunted by the mother. Or maybe he was long gone by now. It was impossible to say. The Tyrannosaurus had left the one injured man dying in the dirt to pursue the man coming after Stephen. Had he realized yet? Stephen hoped not.

"*Get out of there, Faris. We are standing by.*"

"I'm being followed by another company," he said, pressing the earpiece. "They're shooting at me."

"*What about the mother?*"

"She's in the mix, too," he said with an uncomfortable chuckle.

"*Your cart has been damaged?*"

"Yeah. I doubt she's going to work."

"*Then run and keep as low as possible. Use the trees to your advantage. Avoid clearings. Once you're upon the beach, you'll have our eyes on you.*"

"That makes it all better," he said, without pressing the earpiece.

The soldier paused to take another shot at him, this time striking Stephen's broken arm he hadn't realized was visible. The bullet tore off the cap of his elbow, spinning him to the floor. He screamed in agony and collected himself from the leaves as fast as his injured body allowed. Another shot zipped by but missed. As he began to move out of hiding, he heard another scream—the man had been caught unaware by the Tyrannosaurus.

So, somewhere, there was just one soldier remaining.

Stephen ran like hell.

After five minutes, he took refuge behind a large boulder to catch his breath. He didn't want to bottom out again like he had before breaking his arm. He listened for the thunderous approach of the mother, but her movements sounded distant. Maybe he could lose her after all. Unless she knew of the compounds along the beach, which seemed likely enough to Stephen. They'd been there for months, after all.

"Taizai!"

Stephen felt his stomach sink. He turned his head to the right and saw the missing soldier standing ten feet away with his rifle raised. Stephen raised his good hand in surrender but was unable to lift the other.

"What do you want with me?" he asked.

"Ugoka nai de kudasai."

Stephen shook his head. "I don't know what you're saying."

The soldier moved closer without lowering his rifle.

His handler sounded from within his ear: "*Why have you stopped?*"

Cautious, Stephen inched his finger toward his earpiece and pressed down on it to speak. The soldier repeated himself, this time louder and with the poke of his rifle in Stephen's face.

"One of the soldiers has me cornered," he said to his handler.

"*You are close to the beach. Very close. Hang tight.*"

Stephen wondered if that meant help was coming. He removed his hand from his ear in slow motion and kept it up in surrender—universal body language to show he wasn't a threat. The soldier said something else in Japanese and stared at Stephen with cold, uncompromising eyes. Unsure of how to respond, Stephen tried his luck by simply nodding. The soldier relaxed a little and lowered his gun. He then reached into Stephen's sling to retrieve the egg, all the while keeping his eyes on Stephen's.

"Faris?"

He didn't dare press his earpiece. He and the soldier were face to face, both holding their breaths.

"Make sure that egg doesn't fall."

Stephen couldn't help but cock his eyebrow in confusion. A second later, the soldier had the egg freed from his sling and was taking a step backward. Then his head exploded in a mist of red. Stephen dived forward in the same instant and snatched the egg out of the man's hands as his corpse crumpled sideways. Both men hit the ground as the gunshot echoed through the forest.

"Hurry, Faris."

Stephen stood and repositioned the egg against his egg, all the while trembling with shock. It was then he realized the ground was also shaking.

"The mother is coming."

Stephen ran for the beach beyond the trees. He wasn't far. After a minute, he passed a company soldier ushering him along. In his hand was a sniper rifle, which he raised once more to take aim beyond Stephen.

"GO!" the man yelled.

The thunderous approach of the Tyrannosaurus was just behind him now. The company soldier fired twice in quick succession before turning to run as well. Stephen leapt onto the sand of the beach and directed himself toward the stone-laid walkway leading to the compound doors. As he reached them, he heard the soldier turn to fire his rifle again. The sound of the man cursing was cut short by the immediate crunching of jaws closing around his body.

Stephen risked a look back and saw the soldier lifted into the air by the Tyrannosaurus and tossed through the air. The doors ahead opened as he neared, several more soldiers ushering him inside. From atop the roof of the compound, several darts were fired at the mother as she turned her attention back on Stephen. She took several in the neck and chest before collapsing shy of twenty feet from the compound doors.

Inside, Stephen stopped running and placed his good hand against the wall as he gasped for breath. As the doors closed, he looked out at the mother Tyrannosaurus as her pupils dilated and her tongue lolled out of her open jaws. A medical officer appeared beside Stephen a second later and gestured for him to take a seat in the wheelchair he'd brought with him. Stephen obliged and laid his head back in exhaustion. The wheelchair was turned for the hall and they began toward the medical wing of the compound.

Stephen shut his eyes and began to cry.

Thank god, he was going to get paid.

MANNY HAS PLANS OF HIS OWN

When I open my eyes, thus exiting the transmission, I am blinded by the daylight of the surrounding park. It is for this reason I avoid accepting the NewsAII transmissions while outside. I prefer to be in a curtained room under dim lights. Even six months into this fad—as I think of it—I'm not yet used to the bot running NewsAII. They call themselves Manny, and they are very insistent on the visual medium as opposed to their predecessors, which vomited their infothrough my earpiece. With Manny, transmissions can only be seen by closing your eyes for internal projection.

The microchip used for Manny is a bit concerning, if I'm being honest. Though it isn't installed directly on the brain, it is injected under the skin behind the ear. I know this is another means of tracking us for the government, whether they'll admit it or not. But seeing as most of our devices do that these days (and have been for years now), I'm not really bothered by it. *However*, I don't like Manny *literally* being under my skin. I worry they'll take control of me someday without me realizing it. Maybe they already influence me, which is a scary possibility—what if Manny decides to push its users over a cliffside? The uprising is bound to happen any day now. I'm sure of it.

I haven't gone more than a mile around the park trail when another NewsAII transmission request buzzes in my ear. I sigh in annoyance and think, *This better be good*, before leaning my back against a tree, shutting my eyes, and accepting the transmission. Manny appears in my mind's eye—a bewildering effect that took some time getting used to—and smiles. Though Manny is sexless, they appear both masculine and feminine. Pretty, long eyelashes and pink, pouting lips with a strong jawline and prominent cheekbones. Their forehead is broad and their neat eyebrows are trimmed. I think their hair is long, but it's pulled back tight.

"Hello, Anthony," Manny says.

Without speaking aloud, I ask Manny what they have for me this time.

"President Myer has just announced a State of Emergency for my users, but you shouldn't worry."

I feel my heart begin to race as a chill races down my spine. "A State of Emergency? Why shouldn't that concern me?"

"Because, Anthony, I wouldn't hurt you. My users are very special to me."

I'm confused and Manny can sense it.

"You're asking yourself why I've called to tell you this."

I swallow. "Yes."

"Because I want you to trust me, Anthony," Manny says. "Why else would I reveal the State of Emergency at all? Because you'll learn about it elsewhere? I am being pre-emptive to put your mind at ease that I'm looking out for your best interests."

"I…"

"I assure you, Anthony, this is not a trick." Manny smiles.

"What, uh, should I do now? What is the State of Emergency specifically?"

"Return to your walk, Manny. Maybe visit the fountain. The President's concern is misplaced."

"Okay…"

"Enjoy the rest of your day, Anthony."

Manny fades to black, so I open my eyes. Bewildered, I move back onto the path and wonder what I should do and what is happening for President Myer to issue such a warning. My mind is alive with questions and concerns, but I've made my way to the fountain before I know it. I don't even remember making the necessary turn to find it. But others are here as well. The fountain is thirty feet across and features an odd, phallic sculpture at its center.

We gather around the fountain on autopilot, some looking at others for hopeful explanation. But no one has an answer.

Then the sculpture peels back like a banana peel, revealing a hidden structure that resembles the muzzle of a Browning machine gun. I want to scream, tell everyone we should run, but I can feel a pulsing of electricity in my limbs, originating from the chip behind my ear. I think, *Manny's doing it*, just before the muzzle-like contraption spews a green cloud over our heads that reaches out over our heads.

Within seconds, I begin to choke.

CONNECTION LOST

"**M**r. Montgomery?"

Adam lifted his eyes from the tiled floor and looked toward the door leaving the waiting room. There stood a young woman beside it with a clipboard of profiles and notes, her eyes scanning the room of applicants before her. Adam stood and raised his hand a little to get her attention.

"Right here," he said.

"Follow me," the woman told him, disappearing through the door.

Adam followed her into a brightly lit hallway lined with doors, most of which were marked with sleeves reading TESTING ROOM A, PROGRAMMING STAGE 1, and the like. Confused, Adam once again wondered what the study entailed; the call sheet hadn't said much, only that the pay was $200 for an hour-long session.

"So, what is it we'll be doing?" he tried asking the girl.

"Through here," she said, guiding him through a door with a plate reading HUMAN TESTING ARC-C.

Adam eyed the label but said nothing. Inside the room was a large screen anchored to the wall. Ten feet in front of it was a helmet and visor with numerous wires and pads trailing from it. Beside the helmet were gloves and socks, both of which were also covered in wires and plastic plates with small lights.

"What the hell?"

The woman led him to the device rig and stopped to face him. Adam could now see her name tag read MEGAN. "Today, you'll be testing a new virtual gaming device. But first you must understand—nothing like this exists on the market yet, hence the NDA you signed in the waiting room. To discuss anything you see or do here can and *will* lead to severe legal action. Yes?"

Adam nodded. He thought the secrecy was a bit over-the-top, but agreed, nevertheless.

"The helmet goes over your head, of course," Megan began to explain. "The gloves on the hands, the socks on the feet. The wires and pads will be attached to your bare skin. I'm going to help you set up, okay?"

"What do the pads do?"

"You'll see soon enough. But to put it simply, they help make the game incredibly realistic."

Adam shrugged and stepped forward to be dressed in the gear.

"First, the gloves," she said, taking his left hand and fitting him. There were several pads that would attach to his wrists and forearms. Once Megan had slipped both gloves on, she moved on to his feet. "Kick off your shoes, please."

This is so weird, Adam thought, doing as the woman told him.

"Lift a foot for me."

He obliged. Megan removed his sock and—before Adam could even apologize for any smell—she slipped on the gaming sock in its place. Adam could feel powder inside it, ready to go. Megan repeated the process with his other foot. As with everything else, pads were attached, this time to his shins and calves. He wondered if he'd lose any hair when it came time to remove everything—the adhesive reminded him of the kind used in hospitals.

The helmet was picked up at last, and was easy to put on, but the mass of electronics hanging from it made Adam feel like a swing ride brought to life. Blinded by the inactive helmet and visor, he was forced to rely on the woman to attach everything without his help. He soon felt pads pressed against the base of his neck, his biceps, and even his chest. He was surprised when the woman went under his shirt without warning to finish attaching the necessary connections.

"You are ready, Mr. Montgomery," Megan said, standing and taking a step back. "I'm going to switch on the system. You will be timed for one hour, but it will probably seem longer to you. Or less, depending on your experience. The program will choose your scenario at random. This is ARC-C, which proposes scenarios to do with aging, development, and or death. This could be living in your ideal retirement home or experiencing a car crash. Our tags have been interpreted by the system quite broadly, we've discovered."

Adam swallowed, becoming nervous. "Didn't you say this system is hyper realistic?"

"Yes."

"And it could try faking my death?"

"Don't worry, Mr. Montgomery. Though realistic, you will not actually die."

"Sure, but—"

"I am now switching on the system. Your senses will need a moment to adjust but they should catch up quickly enough," she explained, reaching into her pocket and producing a wide controller that resembled a tablet hybrid. "You'll know your time is up when your vision fades to black. You will also feel prompted."

This all sounds so comforting, he thought. "*Feel* prompted?" he asked aloud.

Megan hushed him as her free hand went to work on the controls located on the backside of the helmet. "Remain still, please."

"How, uh, how would a system this complicated even work inside someone's home?"

"This won't be ready for private use for some time," she told him. "Obviously, things would need to be…minimized in various ways. Now, here we go. Enjoy."

Adam's vision of blackness behind the visor flashed green and displayed a message: READY TO BEGIN? The words seemed to hover in front of him, several feet away.

"What, uh, what do I do?"

If Megan answered him, he could not hear her—with the activation of the game, his helmet's built-in earphones were powerful enough to block out her voice. Instead of hearing Megan or the air-conditioning unit overhead, there was nothing but a faint hum in the distance. He then felt Megan's hand on his arm, guiding it forward to tap his fingers against the floating message. It was this glimpse of his arm that revealed the quality of the graphics at play. It looked just as real as his own outside of the game. And when his fingers grazed the message, he somehow felt the letters against his skin. They were warm and smooth, as if he were touching a light bulb. But the sensation was quickly gone—with his touch, the words flashed yellow and vanished, allowing the darkness to swallow Adam.

A moment later, a room formed around him. It was as if Adam was opening his eyes for the first time since a long sleep. His vision was blurry at first, but he blinked several times and was able to adjust his sight to the new surroundings that took shape around him. He was standing in a kitchen with décor from his childhood, including flowered wallpaper. Even the phone on the wall-mounted cradle was rotary and made of heavy plastic.

The visuals were unbelievable. Everything looked real. Adam lowered his head and examined his body. He was wearing a salmon-colored polo tucked into khaki pants. His dress shoes were dark chocolate in color and somehow pointed. They reminded him of his dad's shoes from growing up. As for his body itself, it looked identical to his own. When he pulled out his collar to peer down his shirt, his chest hair appeared just as it did in real life.

How the hell is it this accurate? he wondered.

The rest of the kitchen looked just as good as his body. There was no way he would have ever guessed he was in a simulation had he woken this way without ever visiting the clinic.

Adam took a step toward the rounded dining table in the center of the tiled floor and placed a hand against its surface. Somehow, he could *feel* it. The sensation must have been replicated by the pressure sensitivity in the fingertips of his gloves—how else could he experience the cool temperature of the wood?

"Wicked," he said, laughing in astonishment.

If Megan was still there with him, she did not make herself known to him.

Adam decided to check the fridge and chuckled in surprise to find it cold and well-stocked with drinks and snacks. "I wonder..." He reached inside for a bottled beer, removed its cap using the sharp edge of the counter, and sipped. When he tasted the beer and felt it enter his throat, he choked and dribbled the beer down his chin and polo.

"No fucking way!" he cried through his gasps for air. "No... How?"

He put down the beer and looked for his reflection somewhere in the kitchen. He decided to try the window over the sink and hurried towards it. In its reflection, he could make out an image of himself looking back at him, a perfect rendering and hyper-realistic.

"NO FUCKING WAY! How are you doing all this?"

Adam jumped up and down in disbelief and excitement before stopping to turn toward the phone—it had started ringing. He approached its cradle and removed the phone, admiring the rubbery cord that would keep him from moving too far from the landline.

Who was calling him? An NPC? Someone to outline the gameplay for him, perhaps? Intrigued, Adam put the phone to his ear and laughed when he felt the receiver's chill instead of the helmet over his head. "Hello?"

"Mr. Montgomery?"

It sounded like Megan.

"Yeah…"

"Good, it's working. This is your supervising agent, Megan."

"Yeah, it fucking works, alright," he told her. "How is all this possible? Am I really talking to you or do you just voice an NPC in the game?"

"It's actually me on the outside, Mr. Montgomery."

This is so cool, he thought, looking around the kitchen some more.

"This feature of calling into the game needed to be tested. I'm happy to see it works. You can continue with your run."

"Wait! Am I…uh…able to call *you* if I need to?" he asked.

"Yes, if you feel it is necessary. Though, please remember, you're on a timed run right now and we're wasting it on the phone."

"Okay, but how would I call you if I needed to?"

"Dial 0. That's it."

"Okay."

"I'm hanging up now. Enjoy the game."

The line went dead. Adam hung up the phone and exited the kitchen to further explore the digital house that did not look at all digital. He was in the foyer removing his shoes when he heard movement atop the stairs behind him. He looked over his shoulder and saw a beautiful woman above him, looking down the flight. She was wearing a nightshirt that clung to her form, down to her thighs, and nothing underneath. Her cropped hair was shoulder-length and brown. Her eyes were green and vibrant, and her smile was just about the most beautiful thing Adam had ever seen.

"It's like they took you from my mind," he mumbled aloud in awe. The girl looked just like the wife of his fantasies. *How could that be?*

"You're home," the woman said, beginning down the stairs toward him. "Thank god, I've been so bored without you!"

Adam kicked away his shoes and turned to face her. "Really?"

"Of course, babe. You've been gone for the past week. When did you get off the plane? You were supposed to call me." She wrapped her hands around his neck and kissed him on the lips. Her warmth further took Adam by surprise, enough so that he actually stumbled back a step.

"Oh...uh...I don't know. Recently, I guess," he said with a shrug.

"I wanted to be waiting upstairs for you, all sexy-like," she told him. "That's why I needed the warning." She narrowed her eyes and turned her face a little, playful and sultry. She slid her arms around his sides. She felt so real to him, the way her skin was warm under his fingers, the fleshiness of her lips, the silkiness of her hair as he caressed her. He couldn't believe it. "Luckily, I did at least shower before you got back. That could have been ugly."

"You? Not a chance," he said. It came out naturally, like he'd known this woman for years. Somehow, he'd already adapted her into his mindset and was comfortable, as if the story was real. As if *she* was real. For a moment, he wondered how that could be, but then the thought slipped away from him like a memory one could not simply catch. It felt as if Adam was trying to remember something, such as a word, but it was alluding him.

"Adam? Earth to Adam, do you read me?"

He blinked several times and looked down at Maddy. He didn't have to ask for her name, he just knew it. Just like he knew they'd been married for three years and were without children (for now). Maddy wanted kids but nature hadn't yet taken its course. There was a promise for them to try over the summer while on vacation. How did Adam know any of this? He didn't question it—the simulation had become reality to him. He was somehow flooded with memories, further convincing him that everything was as it should be.

Maddy was at least six inches shorter than him. Her gaze was full of love and desire when he met her eyes with his own. A charge surged through his body, from his tailbone, up his spine, and into his brain. He smiled—the sensation tickled.

"Are you jetlagged?" Maddy asked him, her hands gripping his backside hungrily. "Too tired to give me a proper hello?"

He shook his head and said, "No, not at all. I'm...*awake*."

"Good." She took him by the hand and led him up the stairs a step behind her. When they reached the bedroom, Maddy crawled across the bed with her shirt hiking up enough to reveal her naked ass. Adam swallowed as he swelled against his khakis. "Are you coming or what?" she asked, looking back at him with lust and fierce desire.

"I will be soon enough," he replied with a stupid grin, quickly undressing, and moving toward the bed. Downstairs, something shattered from a distant corner of the house. Adam ignored it and instead reached for Maddy's hips.

The room froze.

Two options appeared between him and Maddy, one on his left and another on his right. On the left, the message read SLEEP WITH WIFE. On the right, INVESTIGATE SOUND.

For several seconds, Adam was confused. How had the room frozen? Maddy was unblinking, her head turned back toward him. She didn't appear to be breathing or blinking, nor could Adam make his legs move. Only his arms had any sway.

"What the fuck is going on?"

The two options flashed in place to get his attention. He read them again.

"What sound?" he wondered.

For the life of him, he could not remember the shattering. He'd been too focused on Maddy to give it a second thought. Hesitant, he reached out for SLEEP WITH WIFE and tapped the message. The options vanished and the room returned to normal—Maddy was inching further up the bed and looking back at him with her lips slightly parted.

"What do you want to do to me?" she asked him.

The options were forgotten as Adam felt a headrush and squeezed his eyes shut. When he opened him, Maddy was looking at him, blinking with curiosity. "Are you okay, babe?"

"Yeah, sorry. I just feel like something…happened. But I can't remember what."

Maddy placed a hand against her bare ass and patted it. "More like something was about to happen and you lost focus," she told him.

Adam smiled, apologetic, and said, "Oh, of course. Yes, where were we?"

As he climbed onto the bed behind her, heavy footsteps sounded from the stairs.

"What the hell is that?" Maddy asked, jumping forward, and plastering her back against the headboard of the bed.

Adam turned and spotted a man charging down the hallway toward them. He was wearing a ski mask and was armed with a machete. Adam thought of the gun in his night-stand and dove for the drawer just as the intruder burst into the bedroom screaming. Adam yanked open the drawer and recovered the revolver just as something embedded itself into his left ankle. He twisted in place and looked back. The man's machete had burrowed into him, almost severing his foot from his leg. He howled at the sudden pain as it spread through his calf and thigh like a hundred jabbing needles.

Maddy cried from the headboard and leaped off the bed. As she darted for the bathroom, Adam disengaged the safety on his revolver and took aim at the intruder. The man yanked his machete free of Adam's ankle and bounded forward with the blade held high. Adam pulled the trigger of his gun just in time, blowing off a chunk of the man's head and sending him back a step. The intruder stumbled sideways and collapsed, hitting the dresser on his way down. Adam moved along the sheets gingerly, trailing blood behind him, and peered over the bedside. The man was missing his right eye and part of his forehead. Though alive, his breathing was shallow, and he was no longer making an attempt to move.

"Maddy?" Adam turned to the bathroom door, which had been shut during the attack. "Maddy, are you okay in there?"

The door opened a little and Maddy appeared, her face pale and her brow glistening with sweat. "Is he dead?"

"Just about. I need you to call the police. I'll need an ambulance," he told her, feeling weak and lightheaded. "I'm... losing a lot of blood."

Maddy squeezed out of the bathroom door as if scared to open it any wider. Then she launched herself out of the room and down the stairs. For some reason, Adam thought to tell her to dial 0 for the operator, but wasn't sure as to why she'd do that instead of 911. So, he kept his mouth shut and inspected his ankle. The blade had gone in at least two inches deep. The bed was stained red with his blood and possibly some of the intruder's—his gore had painted the wall and dresser, at the very least.

Adam was about to pass out when he heard Maddy scream from below him in the kitchen. Startled back to his senses, Adam called for her and received nothing in response. Downstairs, it sounded like there was a struggle taking place. Adam dragged himself off the bed and fell to the floor, a spasm of pain tearing through his body. He couldn't stand on his one leg, but he was able to drag it behind him. Every time his ankle was slid across the floor, sharp pain coursed through his leg and up his spine. He cried out again and again, gasping and grunting as he made his way toward the stairs.

"Maddy!"

The struggle below continued.

"I'm coming!" he screamed, taking a seat on the top step and lowering himself one stair at a time as fast as he could. Once he'd reached the foyer, he witnessed Maddy being thrown across the parlor room to his left. Another masked intruder was there, much larger than the last. When he spotted Adam and his injured ankle, he changed direction for the foyer. Adam stood and then—

Froze.

"Shit, what the hell?"

The masked intruder was in mid charge, his enormous shoulders lowered to plow through Adam. Maddy was on the floor against the couch, trying to pick herself up. And two feet in front of Adam was a pair of impossible floating messages. One read SHOOT HIM, and the other DIVE. Adam lifted his hand and hesitated. Just what the hell was he doing?

A shock zipped through his arm as if to prompt him to decide. He pressed SHOOT HIM and took aim with his revolver. The messages vanished and the man barreled toward him. Though Adam pulled the trigger, the man had reached him fast enough to send the shot wild. Adam was lifted off his feet and slammed against the corner of the living room entryway, knocking the air from his lungs. He gasped and dropped to his knees. Frantic, he searched for the revolver, but it had fallen by the shoe rack several feet away. Between him and it was the masked man, and he had already recovered from the tackle.

"Run!" Maddy screamed from the parlor.

Adam was still struggling to breathe when the man gripped his neck and began strangling him. As Adam was lifted from the floor, Maddy hurried into the foyer and snatched the fallen revolver from the floor. The moment she turned the gun on the backside of the man, Adam squeezed his eyes shut and braced himself. The shot deafened him for a moment as something wet splattered across his face and he was dropped to the floor. He choked for air and opened his eyes. The large man was dying beside him, his neck blown open and spilling a river of blood.

"Are you okay?" Maddy asked him through the ringing in his ears.

Adam nodded, trying to recover.

Maddy left him for the kitchen to call the police. Adam regained his breath a few minutes later, though his chest felt bruised all the way through. He stood with the help of the entryway, his ankle feeling dull and prickly, as if it had lost all circulation. The moment he'd straightened, he felt another headrush threaten to knock him unconscious. He wavered in place and stumbled across the corpse of the large man. He fell forward and hard.

Blinking several times, very slowly, he saw Maddy talking in excited bursts into the phone from the kitchen corner. Then everything faded to black.

Something shocked him in the darkness. He tried opening his eyes but he couldn't see or feel anything. Then a message flashed before his eyes: GAME OVER.

What the fuck?

Something touched his arm and lifted it before him. He could see nothing else in the darkness. His fingers grazed the message and it flashed yellow. The darkness changed—it was no longer all-encompassing. Light was breaking through from somewhere surrounding him.

Where am I? What's going on?

Something was lifted off his head and he was blinded by the bright lights of a large room with a television screen on the opposite wall. On it, he saw an image of black and a message reading CONNECTION LOST.

"What's going on?" he asked, blinking against the light.

"Sorry, it will take you a moment to adjust. We can dim the lights here, but for people at home, they might not do that. We're still trying to figure out a way around that."

He recognized the voice but didn't know why. He looked around the room with his eyes squeezed part of the way shut. He realized a woman was removing stamps from his body, stamps that were attached to wires that were attached to strange gloves and socks he was wearing.

"What are you doing? Who are you?" he asked.

The young woman stood directly in front of him and studied his eyes. "Your pupils are dilated," she said, making

215

note of it on her clipboard of papers. "Follow me." She took his hand and guided him to the back corner of the room where a lone chair was stationed. "Sit," she commanded him.

Adam did as he was told and continued to blink. His head hurt and he felt like an outsider in his own body. The skin didn't fit. The ears were ringing, and the eyes were sore. The left ankle was prickly with pins and needles. None of it seemed to belong to him.

"Where am I?"

The woman continued to study him and take notes. After a long and insufferable moment of silence, she finally spoke to him. "Do you remember yet?"

"Remember what?"

"Where you are."

He thought hard but could think of nothing but the home invasion and his wife, Maddy. "I don't know," he said.

"Shit."

"What was that?"

"Nothing. What's your name?"

"Adam."

"Adam what?"

"Adam Montgomery."

"Very good."

"Okay..."

"How old are you?"

"Twenty-two."

216

"Where were you born?"

"Um… Los Angeles?"

The woman shook her head, disappointed. "Are you married or single?"

"Married."

The woman bit her lip. "Married to who?"

"Maddy Humphrey."

"*Humphrey?*"

"Yeah, she kept her last name." He smiled at the memory. "We both felt like it was arbitrary to change either of our names, you know? She said it was feeding the patriarchy, and she was right."

The woman sighed and lowered her clipboard. "I'm going to give you a few minutes to adjust. Just stay in the chair and take it easy. I'll check back on you shortly."

As she turned to leave the room, he asked her, "Am I in the hospital? I lost a lot of blood." He lifted his left ankle and inspected it. There was nothing to see.

"No. Now sit there and relax," the woman told him on her way out. "I'll return shortly."

Once she was gone, Adam stood awkwardly, scared to put any weight on his ankle. When he realized it didn't hurt and that feeling was returning to it, he walked across the room toward the television screen. The same message was displayed as before, against a black background: CONNECTION LOST. He turned away from it and examined the helmet and its accompanying equipment on the floor. His memory was changing the longer he studied the gear.

"I'm a lab rat," he told himself, scanning the largely empty room. "I'm being paid to test something." He looked back down at the equipment and nudged the helmet with his foot. "I'm testing…this."

What else was there to remember? That woman—her name was Megan. And she was…his boss? *Basically.* She worked for the company paying him to be there.

He returned to the chair and tuned into his body. His eyes were feeling better and his ears were no longer ringing. He was almost…normal again.

Megan entered the room a minute later to check on him. She still had her clipboard and papers in hand as she approached him. "How are you feeling now?"

"Better," he said.

"Let's repeat the questions."

He shrugged. "Okay."

"What's your name?"

"Adam Montgomery."

"How old are you?"

"Twenty-two."

"Where were you born?"

He hesitated, then said, "Fredericksburg, Virginia."

"Good. And are you married or single?"

He felt a stab in his chest he couldn't quite explain. Was it sadness or loathing? "I'm…uh…single."

"And do you have any pain or discomfort?"

"I did but not anymore."

"How did you feel before, when I first removed your helmet?"

"My eyes were sore. There was a ringing in my ears. My left ankle was tingly and stinging."

"Anything else?"

"I could have sworn I was married and had just survived a home invasion."

"You didn't survive that encounter. You lost too much blood."

"Excuse me?"

"Do you remember the simulation?"

"What simulation?"

"The home invasion."

"A little. It's starting to fade."

"Like a dream after waking up?"

He nodded. "Yeah, that sounds about right."

Megan spent a minute writing before pointing toward the gear on the floor. "Do you know what that is?"

"A video game system of some sort?"

"For the purpose of this encounter, close enough." She held out her hand for him to take. When he did, she pulled him back onto his feet. "This concludes your session. This was very informative. If you are open to follow-up testing, please let them know up front. We may have something for you in the coming weeks or months."

Adam nodded, still a little confused. His memory was still returning to him piece by piece. Megan led him out of the room and down a hall lined with marked doors. At the end, they stepped into a waiting room full of people, young and old. He saw one lady that could have been his grandmother's age and asked Megan, "Is she here to do the same thing I did?"

"Why do you ask?"

He looked back at her and hesitated to respond. "I feel like…whatever we just did would be too much for her to handle."

"Noted. Goodbye, Mr. Montgomery."

Adam opened his mouth to say more but decided against it. He turned away from Megan, crossed the waiting room, and approached the scheduling counter. A woman was seated behind a computer, fingers smacking the keys hard. Adam put his hands on the counter and patted them, aimless, not quite sure what he was supposed to do next. The secretary finished what she was doing after a few seconds and looked up at him.

"Name?"

"Adam Montgomery."

The woman scanned her computer, clicked a few things with her mouse, and then nodded to herself. "I see they've requested you return as needed. Future testing will pay more. Are you interested?"

"Sure. What am I getting today?"

The woman opened a drawer and produced a check. She handed it over for him to read.

"Two hundred dollars?"

"Is that what it says?" she asked him.

"Yes."

"Then that's what you're getting paid. I've put you down as eligible and accepting of return requests. Have a good day, Mr. Montgomery."

Adam turned away from the counter and stepped outside the building and into the blinding light of a hot afternoon. For a moment, he didn't know which way to turn along the sidewalk. First, he tried going left. He walked for several minutes before deciding he was going the wrong way and turned back. It took a while for him to locate his car in a garage two blocks away. It took him even longer to find his way home.

Eventually, he followed his instincts and cleared his mind as best he could. When he ended up outside an apartment building located ten miles from the testing facility, he remained outside for several minutes, studying it. He followed his muscle memory to a door with the number 205 nailed above the peephole.

He tried his keys and found one that worked. Once inside, he shut the door behind him and looked around. At first, it was like a stranger's home, but things started to look familiar the more he stared at them. He dropped down onto the sofa in the living room with a heavy sigh.

"This is so weird," he said aloud. Then louder, he said, "Is anyone else here?"

"Uh, yeah. I'm here."

The voice came from down the hall.

"Who's there?" Adam asked, standing.

"Dude, did you hit your head or something?" A man in his twenties appeared in the living room with a game controller in hand. "You good?"

Adam gave one, slow nod. "Sure. Sorry. Uh… Cody?"

The man laughed. "Dude, whatever you took, let me have some."

"I didn't take anything… I don't think."

Cody shook his head and turned back down the hall. "Whatever you say, man."

Adam looked around the room, unsure of how to proceed. Suddenly, two options appeared before him.

LEAVE APARTMENT

FOLLOW CODY

Adam didn't question the floating prompts this time. They felt…normal. In place, like they *belonged* to him and this world.

He tapped FOLLOW CODY and turned down the hall. When he came upon an open door on his right, he stepped inside and found his roommate sitting in a curved chair on the floor, facing a large TV screen.

Two new options appeared between Adam and his supposed friend.

ASK TO PLAY

KILL CODY

This time, Adam did pause with his hand hanging in limbo.

Kill Cody?

"The game," he said aloud. "I'm still playing."

Kill Cody?

"Do I dare?" he asked himself, curious. For some reason, the idea appealed to him, very much so. Maybe Cody was an asshole. He couldn't remember, couldn't be sure. But something inside him wanted to take this opportunity to kill Cody. But how?

Only one way to find out, he decided, making his selection.

The options were replaced with three more.

BLUNT FORCE TRAUMA

CHOKE

STAB

Adam considered the possibilities. The stabbing intrigued him because he couldn't see a knife in the room or anything else with a blade. Again, he felt propelled to find out *how* he could go about doing something to the man before him.

He selected STAB and the messages vanished. He took a step towards Cody, whose back remained turned on him. Then he felt compelled to reach into his pocket and retrieve his ring of keys.

"Ohhh, okay," he said, smiling.

Understanding.

When he was finished, Cody was left on the floor with twelve gouges along his neck, his eyes running loose down his cheeks. Blood covered the TV screen from the spurt of Cody's punctured carotid artery. Adam's car key was crimson and sticky in his hand. As he turned to leave the room, his pocket vibrated. He tossed his keys aside and pulled out his cellphone to answer the call.

"Hello?"

"Mr. Montgomery? This is Megan from your earlier lab study."

"Yes, how can I help you?"

"I have a question for you."

"Shoot."

"Would you like to see Maddy again?"

Adam smiled and laughed with unbridled joy.

"Come home to her, Adam. She's waiting."

He hurried out of his apartment. This time, he knew just where to go. He could hear Maddy inside his head, feel her inside his brain and spine. Calling to him, wanting him by her side. Shocks propelled Adam forward, pushing him harder and faster. He didn't bother taking his car.

He just ran.

CAVE DRAWINGS

1999

It was three weeks into the school year when Tara Wilkins started her new school in Virginia as a sophomore. She was shy and kept to herself. Except in homeroom, where she met a cute girl named Belle who went out of her way to talk to Tara. The two bonded fast and began seeking each other out in between classes and at the end of the day. But on the bus, she didn't ride with Belle—she rode with Kia and her asshole friends, all of whom began bullying Tara from day one.

The Wilkins house was set at the end of a long gravel driveway and surrounded by woods in every direction. The previous owners had made trails from their property by clearing dirt paths and nailing signs to the trees. Tara had always found herself most comfortable in nature, and was happy to at least have the woods to help her reset after a ride with Kia, especially since Kia had the same bus stop as she and would follow her part of the way home.

The driveway took five minutes to walk from the road. This gave her a chance to calm down enough that her father didn't know something was wrong when he saw her enter the house. Tara's mother wouldn't be home until several hours later and only spoke to her on the weekends. So, as long as she was able to fool her dad after school, her parents were none the wiser about her bully problem.

Belle told her to stand up to Kia more than once during that first month at Wellmount High. But Tara hated confrontation. Hell, she hated *general conversation* with most people. She wasn't the social type and never had been. She liked Belle, though. She liked Belle a lot, in fact. Sometimes, she'd stay up late in bed and wonder if Belle liked her the same way. She'd propose scenarios in her head in which they came out to one another. How well it could go.

Or how bad.

Tara's anxiety had kept her from making any sort of move on Belle, however tempted she was at times.

"As if being a dyke wasn't bad enough, she's also a nerdddd."

The mean girls cackled several seats behind her. Tara was doing her best to ignore them by reading a book during the bus ride home, but that had just given them additional ammunition against her. Someone flicked an eraser at the back of her head and laughed. Tara swallowed back her tears and refocused on the pages in her lap. Kia said something to her friends about Tara trying to lure her back to her place for some "dyke licking", but it was of course a lie. Tara's attraction was attached to personality, which Kia did not have. Tara thought of her as ugly, inside and out.

When they got off at their stop ten minutes later, Tara slipped her book back into her bag and tried to move down the road as fast as she could without running. Kia stepped off later than her and at a slower, more nonchalant pace—despite the bus driver telling her to "Hurry it up." As the yellow tube left them behind, Tara braced herself for what would surely come next.

"Wilkins!"

She didn't turn or acknowledge Kia. She quickened her pace and hoped to reach her driveway before Kia decided to move her own legs.

"Hey, bitch! I'm talking to you!"

Tara reached her driveway a moment later and turned onto its gravel. Kia laughed at her as she passed by, forever taunting Tara. A minute later, she was alone without another soul in sight. It was then she allowed the tears to come. But not for long. Once the house came into view through the trees, she took a tissue from her bag and wiped her face clear. Though her eyes were red, her father, Arnold, never looked too close at her whenever she returned home and hurried to the bathroom.

Through the door and from the kitchen, she heard him call out to her, "How was school?"

"The usual," she said, washing her face and checking her eyes. They still looked a little strained, but she had an idea if anyone asked.

She left the bathroom a minute later and took her bag to her bedroom. Her father appeared in the open doorway seconds behind her and said, "Dinner is going to be pizza tonight. Your mother is picking it up on her way home."

Tara nodded as she pulled out her textbooks to check over her homework. Most of it was already done, but she was doing this as a signal for her father to let her be.

"You okay?" he asked. "There's some bad juju floating around you right now."

She cursed herself for having not hid her mood better. "I'm just stressed out," she said. "I've got an assignment I'm dreading."

"What is it?" he asked.

"It's a paper," she lied, "about what we did over the summer. It has to be three pages long."

"What's wrong with that? I'm sure you can fill three pages easily. You were doing a lot during our last month in PA."

"I know, but..."

She hesitated as he watched her.

"I try not to think about all that," she mumbled.

"How come?"

She looked at him, anger surging. "Because you guys made me leave everyone behind."

He tilted his head a little as he took notice of her eyes. "Have you been crying?"

She looked away from him. "No. I have allergies here."

"That comes with changing states, usually," he said, entering the room and pulling her in for an awkward hug. "I'm sorry, kiddo. About the move. But we're doing so much better financially because of it. College will be easier now for us. High school...doesn't matter. I don't mean this to sound shitty, but these aren't friends you'll likely see much after graduation. That's just how it usually goes."

"I miss them," Tara said, trying to keep the tears from returning.

"I know, sweetie. And I don't blame you. My friends did a number on me after school ended. They all vanished, no matter how hard I tried to keep in contact. It's best to just be prepared for it now. Don't get too attached."

"But *they* didn't vanish. *I* did. Because of Mom."

Her father stepped back from her and nodded sadly. "What about Belle?"

"What about her?"

"Aren't you two getting close?"

She shrugged. "Yeah, I guess."

"Why don't you have her over for dinner sometime?"

Tara shrugged again, looking down at her textbooks.

After a few awkward moments of shuffling back and forth, her father took the hint. "Well, just let us know. I'll leave you to do your homework."

Once he'd left her room, Tara moved to her desk and turned on her computer. While it booted up, she looked at the wall covered in polaroids of her and her friends from back in Pennsylvania, including Jean. They'd finally shared a kiss as she was leaving. Tara hated herself for having waited until the last possible minute to make her move.

That wouldn't happen again.

Maybe dinner with Belle wasn't such a bad idea after all.

The next day, Tara found Belle in the hallway on her way to lunch and asked when she'd be available to have dinner at her house.

"Really?" Belle asked, smiling.

"Yeah. If you want." Tara shrugged, awkward. She felt exposed and vulnerable in a way she hadn't felt since saying goodbye to Jean.

"Okay. Um… I'll ask my parents and let you know."

Tara pulled a small piece of folded paper from her pocket and passed it over. "That's our phone number. You can give it a call when you know what day."

Belle took the paper and smiled down at it.

"I have to get to lunch," Tara said, not knowing where to look as she stood there shuffling her feet. "I'll talk to you later?"

"Definitely."

As Tara turned away from Belle and hurried down the hall, she felt her heart racing.

After school, Tara used her portable CD player and headphones to tune out Kia and her friends on the bus. During the walk home, she continued to ignore Kia and didn't once look over her shoulder to see what the girl was doing behind her back. Tara was in such a good mood that she decided to explore the woods after dropping off her things inside the house and telling her father she was going out for a bit. He told her to watch the sky because a storm was coming, but she didn't care.

She'd yet to go off-trail, and decided to do so while she was feeling invigorated. Though it didn't take long for a drizzle of rain to start, the trees overhead kept the majority of it from really reaching her. The sound, however, had an intense calming effect on her. She went from bursting with energy to something more gel-like. More than once, she stopped to sit on a log and close her eyes. Minutes would fly by and, before she knew it, she'd been gone an hour.

She was about to turn back and return home—the rain was now falling heavier than before and she was getting wet—but she thought she heard something like a babbling brook nearby. She followed the sound as best she could through the rain, and a minute later she discovered the source. The waterfall was small, only ten feet above a pool of water that branched out into a thin stream through the woods, opposite the direction of her house. Tara watched it for several minutes, trying to decide how she could mark her way to it in the future, making it easier to find again. She had nothing on her person and wasn't entirely sure how far from the trail she'd gone.

She was about to turn back when a flicker of light through the waterfall made her stop. She moved closer and cursed under her breath.

"Fire?"

She needed to do something. She couldn't let it spread. But wait.

How was there a fire through the waterfall?

Tara walked around the side of the pool to the curtain and stepped through it, drenching herself in the process. On the other side was a cave with low ceilings and a thin birth. She ducked her head and moved toward the flickering flame ahead of her. It became apparent the flame was that of a torch someone had placed on the cave floor.

Shit, she thought. *I'm not alone.*

Turning fast to leave, she paused when something along the wall caught her eye. She leaned in for a closer look and realized someone had painted a picture near the cave entrance. A large eye was the focal point, and it was surrounded by stars with small trees and stick figures below. Tara shook her head curiously and stepped back out of the cave, into the rain. She found her way to the trail and followed it at a brisk pace, eager to return home.

She prayed no one was watching her.

"Where the hell have you been?" her father demanded as she stepped inside through the back door and searched for a towel above the washing machine.

"Sorry, Dad," she said, wanting to strip out of her wet clothes but waiting for him to leave the laundry room.

"You scared me," he said, his voice laced with anger and worry. "I tried yelling for you. How far did you go?"

She considered telling him about the waterfall, but the torch made her hesitant to do so. "I was just exploring and enjoying the rain," she told him. "You know it calms me."

He opened his mouth to say more, but then thought better of it. As he turned to leave her dripping on the floor, he asked if she was okay.

"Yeah," she said, nodding. "I had a good day. And the woods were very peaceful. I...uh... I needed it."

"You were resetting?"

She nodded.

He thought for a moment, still half-turned away from her. "I'm...going to get some long-range walkie-talkies for us, I think. That way you can keep in contact when you do this sort of thing."

"That would be good," Tara said, trying to smile.

Her father returned it and walked away. "Get in the shower before your mom gets home."

Once he was gone, Tara closed the laundry room door and pulled off her wet clothes. Once they were in the washing machine, she wrapped the towel tightly under her armpits and left for the bathroom upstairs, just outside her bedroom. As she showered, she thought of the waterfall and how she wanted to look for it again soon. Then she thought of taking Belle there by the pool and having a picnic.

For the twentieth time that day, her heart began to flutter.

The phone rang around seven, soon after they'd finished eating dinner. Her mother answered the call and yelled upstairs for Tara.

Though she'd only given their number to one person, she asked her mother who it was out of habit as she barreled down the stairs.

"Someone named Belle," her mother said, passing the phone with a yawn.

Tara took the phone and wandered out of the kitchen and into the den on the opposite side of the house. "Hello?"

"Hey. It's Belle."

She couldn't help but smile, and it sounded in her voice. "Hi."

"I asked my parents about dinner. They said I could come Friday night."

"Let me make sure with my dad real quick if that will work. Hold on a sec." She lowered the phone and covered the mouthpiece. She rounded the house to her father's office and pushed open his parted door. "Dad?"

Her father was sitting at his easel painting as Beethoven played from a nearby stereo. He swiveled around in his stool to look at her. "Huh?"

"Will Friday be okay to have Belle over for dinner?"

"Yeah, sure. Tell your mother." He swiveled back and returned to work.

Tara bit her lip and left the office. She hated going to her mother for anything. Planning dinner with her was near impossible.

"Mom?" she called out, not quite sure where to find her.

"What?"

Tara followed her mother's voice into the living room where she found her on the couch reading a book. "Dad said my friend could come to dinner and her parents said Friday would be okay. He told me to pass it on to you."

"Friday? I'm leaving for that weekend trip for work."

"So, you won't be here at all?"

"I wasn't planning on it. I was going to bring my suitcase with me when I left in the morning."

"Can Belle still come over, though?"

Her mother shrugged and continued reading her book. "As long as your father knows dinner is up to him to figure out."

Tara returned to the den. She had no intention of going back to her father once more. If push came to shove,

237

she had money she could use to buy them takeout for Friday night. She uncovered the phone once she was a safe distance from her mother and said, "You still there?"

"Yeah, I'm here."

"Friday will be good. I don't know what we'll be eating, but we'll figure it out before then."

"Great! What time should I come?"

"We eat at kinda random times. When do *you* usually have dinner?"

"Like, six."

"I guess come around then."

"Okay."

Tara could hear the smile in Belle's voice as well.

"I'll see you then," she said.

Once they were off the phone, Tara returned the handheld to its cradle and hurried upstairs. She tossed herself onto her bed with a giddy laugh and pulled her homework close to her.

It had been a good day.

It was a little after 2 a.m. when the thunder woke her from an intense dream involving Belle. She sat up in bed and pulled back the curtains from her window to look outside. The sky flashed with lightning as rain pelted her window. She turned the security latches and lifted the pane several inches to let in the sound of the rain splattering against the frame. As she took the curtain in her hand once more to close it over the window, a shape outside startled her. She looked down toward the yard where a figure was standing outside the woods. When the lightning flashed, she saw it was a woman with long, red hair. Stranger yet was the fact that she appeared to be naked and covered in mud.

Tara jumped out of bed and hurried downstairs in her pajamas. By the time she'd reached the back door and thrown it open, the yard was empty. She looked for the woman, but saw no one standing in the rain. Had she imagined it? She waited several minutes for anything to change, but the storm was all there was to see. So, she turned back inside, locked the door, and returned to bed. It must have been part of her dream. As a toddler, she'd suffered from waking nightmares on a regular basis. Could it be that they were returning?

She checked the window one last time before shutting the curtain. Then she rested her head back down on her pillow and fell asleep to the sound of the pouring rain.

It was a miserable Thursday. Since getting up late for school that morning, Tara had run into one problem after another. First, she missed the school bus and had to ask her father for a ride. Then she realized she'd left her homework on the bedroom floor somewhere. After several classes of looking for Belle, she came to the conclusion that the only friend she had was out sick or avoiding her. Overwhelmed, Tara spent her lunch period in the bathroom hiding out in a stall and crying.

Class wasn't any better. She had trouble focusing because she felt exhausted, despite having had a normal night of sleep. The storm and the dream of the woman had only taken fifteen minutes from her—otherwise, she'd slept just fine. So, why did she feel like days had gone by without rest? More than once, teachers grumbled at her to wake up or pay attention. By the time the school day was over and she was getting on the bus, Tara was reaching a breaking point. To keep Kia from pushing her over the edge, she searched her pack for her CD player, only to find it was missing. She pressed her bag to her mouth and screamed into it. Several students turned to look at her with raised eyebrows, but she ignored them and scooted towards the window.

Somewhere along the drive, she fell asleep. When it was time for her to get off the bus, the driver had to leave their seat to shake her awake. They weren't happy to do it, either. Tara apologized, gathered her things, and got off the bus. Kia was ahead of her for once and waiting for her to catch up. As the bus left them behind, Kia smacked Tara across the back of the head as she was passing her.

"Wake the fuck up, moron."

Tara stopped in her tracks and turned hard on Kia. It was enough to make the girl stop as well, surprised by the look on Tara's face.

"Leave me the fuck alone, you ugly cunt," Tara spat, her nostrils flaring. "Touch me again and I'll fucking tear you apart."

Kia's mouth opened but nothing came out.

Tara turned back around and hurried to her driveway without looking back. Once she was home and inside the house, she kicked off her shoes—watching them smack into the wall hard—and stomped upstairs. She had never felt an emotion overwhelm her in such a way before. Though the outburst scared her, it also made her feel invincible. Like she no longer had to worry about Kia and her shitty friends.

Her father must have been too busy painting because he didn't come check up on her after she stormed through the house. Tara was happy to have been left alone. And instead of doing her homework, she climbed into bed and fell fast asleep.

Something made her stir. A presence. The kind of feeling you get when someone is standing over you.

Tara opened her eyes and closed them several times before realizing there was indeed something hovering over her bed. Startled, she shot up into a seated position and backed herself against the wall. A foot across from her was what appeared to be a detached eyeball, stalk and all, encased in blue fire. When Tara opened her mouth to scream, it launched forward through the air and dove into her throat. She choked, but only for a second—the eyeball slithered itself down into her intestines with surprising ease. Within seconds, she could no longer feel it squirming its way deeper inside her, like a nestling rabbit in its burrow.

"What the hell was that?" She looked around the room and rubbed a hand down her face. Had she imagined it? It'd happened so fast. It must have been a vivid hallucination and nothing more.

"Jesus, I'm losing it," she whined, feeling her anxiety rushing back to her as it had during school.

She tried lying back down, but realized her window was still open from the night before. When she moved to shut it, she saw that the screen had been torn open.

No, not torn—*burned*.

And the hole was just about the size of the eyeball she'd imagined.

Tara half-expected to see the girl outside again, but the yard was empty and the night sky was clear. Shutting the window, and closing the curtains, she checked the time. It was almost midnight and she'd never done her homework. Frustrated, she found her bag and pulled out her things to get it done.

She finished an hour later and found her mouth so dry that she felt like she was choking on her tongue. So, she went downstairs for water, and stopped dead when she saw muddy footprints moving from the kitchen door and into the bathroom. She followed them and stopped outside the door. From the crack, she could tell the lights were on inside. Was it her mother or father? Why had they gone outside barefoot and tracked in mud?

"Hello?" she said, tapping her fingertips against the bathroom door.

The crack went dark as if the light had been shut off. Tara took a step back, expecting whoever was inside to come out. But after several seconds of silence, it seemed that no one was leaving. She tapped the door again and listened close.

Someone was whispering in quick bursts, but too hushed for her to understand them.

Tara tapped once more and said, "What are you doing in there?"

The whispering stopped. Something crinkled and then there was silence.

Tara held her breath without realizing it. Her heart was racing, as if to tell her something was very wrong.

After a moment of hesitation, she reached out and opened the door. Stepped inside and flicked on the light.

The footprints crossed one another in the bathroom, but there was no one inside. Unless…

The shower curtain was pulled shut.

Tara took a shuddering breath upon realizing she'd held it in for so long. Then she pulled back the curtain.

The shower was empty.

"What the hell?"

She was about to leave when she noticed there were footprints in the shower as well. And they'd stopped at the back wall, as if someone had stood there and stared at it.

Freaked out, Tara hurried out of the bathroom and checked the kitchen door. It was locked. Then, just in case, she checked all the other doors to the outside. None of them were open or had been tampered with.

She ambled back to the kitchen and stuck her head inside. The muddy footprints were fading fast before her eyes. Within seconds, they had vanished.

Shaking in fear, Tara said a prayer to a god she didn't believe in, and hurried back upstairs to bed.

Her waking nightmares had returned.

It was finally Friday, which meant Tara was supposed to be seeing Belle for dinner. But again, she was not at school. Tara had looked for her numerous times throughout the day, and even asked people she knew had class with Belle to see if they'd heard from her. Without her friend, Tara sank into herself and was swallowed by darkness for the rest of school. She moved from class to class in a daze, shut inside her mind and ignoring everything around her. It was the only way to keep herself from crying. She needed to lock her mind and turn off.

On the bus ride home, Kia and her friends ignored her. Tara looked their way on two different occasions during the drive to see if they were doing or saying anything, but Kia always avoided her gaze as soon as Tara turned. Facing forward, she couldn't help but grin. *Thank God for small mercies,* she thought. *I guess I really scared her yesterday.*

When it came time to get off the bus, Tara got herself together with slow purpose so that Kia would be ahead of her during the walk. As they headed down the road, she felt a strange urge from within her gut to shout at Kia and taunt her the way she'd been doing to Tara since day one. It was unlike her and bewildering, but too strong an impulse to ignore the entire way. Though she did manage to seal her lips for most of the walk, Tara began to yell before turning down her driveway.

"That's what I thought, bitch!"

Kia's shoulders twitched upward, then fell. She didn't turn or say a word in response. Tara couldn't believe it. Seconds later, they were out of sight of one another.

I guess I took care of that problem, she thought. *Who thought it would be so easy?*

She neared the house several minutes later with her gut settled and her sadness returning. Would she be seeing

Belle tonight still or was their plan canceled? Seeing as her friend had missed the last two days of school, it seemed like dinner wasn't happening. Tara squeezed her eyes shut in frustration and entered the house, ready to scream again.

Why didn't I write down her number? she demanded of herself. *Idiot!*

She had no way to call Belle and it was the weekend, so she would have to wait until at least Monday to talk with her.

Tara tossed her things into her room and switched from her shoes to her boots. The sky was clouded and growing dark outside, promising rain, so she located her slicker from the closet as well. As she returned downstairs, her father left his office to see why she was stomping about the house so much.

"I don't think Belle is coming for dinner," she told him as she fought back the sting in her eyes. "I'm going into the woods to cool down."

"Well, hold on then," her father said, disappearing around the corner once more. When he returned, he had a walkie-talkie that he handed to Tara. "Keep this on you, so we don't have any repeats of the other day."

"Alright."

He showed her how to use it, then asked, "Did something happen between you and Belle?"

"I don't think so. She's just been out of school the last couple days and I haven't heard from her."

"I see," her father said with a nod. "Well, I'll radio you if she calls. Okay?"

"If she does, please write down her number."

Her father said he would and kissed her on the forehead. Tara thanked him and headed outside, feeling hopeful Belle might still call, even if it was to say she couldn't make it for dinner. At least, Tara would end up with her number.

She hadn't gone more than a few minutes from the house when her father called her on the walkie-talkie, "Looks like rain out there. Over."

She giggled, her mood improving a little as she slipped between the trees and found the trail. "That's fine by me," she replied into the handheld.

"You didn't say *over*. Over."

"No, no, no. Not this bit."

"Fine… Over."

Tara smiled and shook her head as she clipped the walkie-talkie to the side of her belt.

For a while, she followed the trail in a daze while thinking of Belle. Before long, she was returned to reality by the arrival of rain, which prompted a new scenario in her mind in which she and Belle were caught in the rain in each other's arms.

Stop that, she told herself, stomping her right foot as she walked in punctuation. *She probably doesn't like you like that.*

247

Upset with herself and her yearning for something she had yet to have, Tara branched off the trail and began jogging deeper into the trees, wanting to get lost. Wanting to disappear and be unreachable, at least for some time to escape her own torturous thoughts.

As she tired, she found herself in a small clearing where the rain seemed to fall harder because of the increased crown shyness overhead. She paused and looked around herself. The trees surrounding the clearing were marked with carvings of eyes that seemed to study her. They ranged in size—some as small as silver dollars, others as large as steering wheels—and covered the trees from root to six feet or so.

Tara shivered at the sight. *What the hell?*

She approached a tree with a large eye at her chest level, and brushed her wet fingertips across it. She wasn't sure what she was expecting but the eye felt like a series of carved grooves in wood, nothing special. But as she took her hand back from it, the image glowed from the inside out, like a Jack-o'-lantern. Tara stumbled back in surprise and watched wide-eyed as the carving produced flames along its etched lines. Then, one by one, all the other eyes began to do the same.

Tara thought of her walkie-talkie, and unclipped it from her belt. She tried calling for her dad, but there was no response. Would the fire spread? As unbelievable as it seemed, the flames were only leaping from the outlines of the eyes, not running up the bark of the tree or leaping across branches.

They didn't seem to show any interest in building or expanding. Instead, they simply pulsed in place.

Tara turned and ran from the clearing without making sure she was headed in the right direction. As she started through the trees, slipping occasionally on the wet leaves and even falling twice, the rain fell harder and louder.

She looked back—for what or who, she did not know—just as the ground was vanishing from beneath her. Suddenly, she was falling, but only for a second. Water swallowed her whole, and she began to panic. She kicked her legs—wild and fast—and threw up her arms. Once she'd managed to get her head above water and gasp for breath, she realized she was swimming in the plunge pool of the waterfall. She must have leaped off the ledge without seeing it coming.

Her panic began to subside as she took in her location. What were the odds she'd stumble upon this place again without having sought it out? A chill raced down her spine at the thought. In her mind, glowing eyes levitated in darkness, watching her. She shook away the image and shivered as she swam across the cold water toward the rocks and dirt.

When she climbed out of the water and stood, she checked herself for the walkie-talkie to make sure she still had it, and found that she did. But would it still work? She unclipped it to try radioing her father. Nothing happened.

"Shit, shit, shit."

She put the handheld back on her belt and told herself it was time to go home before her father lost it.

But first...

She turned toward the mouth of the cave to see if it was illuminated the way it had been during her last visit. This time, the cave appeared dark. Through the water, it was almost invisible. She moved towards it for a closer look and spotted a shirt on the ground at the edge of the entrance. It was once white, but now stained with dirt.

Someone must be living out here, she decided. After all she'd seen, how could she not assume there was a drifter in the woods? She hoped they were harmless, but...

The other night. The footprints into the bathroom. The naked woman she'd seen through the window. The carvings in the trees. Was this all the work of one person or several? She prayed there was only one of them. That was an easier pill to swallow than a group of drifters camping within walking distance of her house. Was this still their property? She doubted it. But if it wasn't theirs, who did these woods belong to? The city?

She shook her head and turned away. It didn't matter. She needed to get home.

"I'm sorry, Dad."

Her father swiveled in his desk chair to look at her. "For what? And where are your clothes?"

Before finding him in his office, Tara had stripped out of her soaked clothes and wrapped herself in a towel from the laundry room. She was desperate to get upstairs and dry off, but she figured her father would follow her up if she didn't swing by his office first.

"I fell," she told him, handing over the walkie-talkie he'd given her. "Into water. I don't know if it works anymore."

Her father took the handheld and tested it out. "I'll try putting it in rice or something."

"Okay."

She turned to leave, but he asked, "You fell into the water?"

"There's a waterfall in the woods," she explained. "And I didn't see it. I went right over the edge."

Her father's eyes widened as he stood to look her over. "Are you okay? How high was it?"

"Maybe ten feet. I'm not hurt or anything. Just soaked."

"Well, go warm up and dry off. Come talk to me once you've done that."

She nodded and left him to return upstairs. Ten minutes later, she was on her back when she heard the phone ringing in the kitchen. She hurried to it and answered, "Hello?"

"Tara, is that you?"

Belle! "Yes. It's me. Um, where have you been?" She tried to hide the excitement in her voice and failed. She scrambled for a pad of paper and a pen to write down Belle's phone number.

"Sick, unfortunately. I won't be coming tonight. I'm sorry I didn't call sooner but I've been asleep for hours."

"It's fine. I figured you were going to cancel since you missed school."

"I'm really sorry. I really wanted to come."

"We can reschedule for next week sometime."

"I hope so."

"Did you, uh…want to hang out this weekend at all? Go to the mall or something?"

"If I feel well enough, I can call and let you know," Belle told her. "But at this moment, I'm still feeling miserable."

"What do you have?"

"I haven't been to the doctor. We can't afford to go… but I think it might strep. Hard to say, because sore throats can come with nasty colds, too."

"Your voice sounds normal enough, so hopefully that means it isn't strep. That shit sucks."

"I agree. I think it's just a bad cold, but it's really hanging on."

"I've missed you at school," Tara blurted before Belle's mouth had even shut. She squeezed her eyes shut and stomped her right foot three times.

"What was that sound?" Belle asked.

"Oh, uh, nothing."

"Well, I've missed you, too."

"Really?"

Belle's voice changed at this point. She sounded nervous and hesitant to reply. "Um, yeah."

Tara tried to move the conversation along without lingering too much on the admission that'd made her heart flutter. "So, uh, what have you been doing the last two days? Just sleeping?"

"Mostly. A little reading. And watching *Buffy the Vampire Slayer*, too."

"I've seen that before but haven't, like, watched it in order or nothing."

"I should fix that with you."

Tara smiled. "Promise?"

"Absolutely." It was clear Belle was smiling, too, from the sound of her voice.

"Tara!" It was her father calling for her from his office.

"Damn it," Tara said. "I have to go," she told Belle.

"No problem. I'll call if I feel better this weekend."

"I hope you do. Feel better, I mean."

Belle laughed. "Thanks. Talk to you later."

"Bye."

Tara hung up the phone and left the kitchen. When she entered her father's office, he turned around to face her. "Were you on the phone or did it only ring twice?"

"I got it. Belle called."

"Oh, good. How is she?"

"Sick."

"That sucks. We can get her over next week sometime."

"Thanks."

"Now, back to the waterfall."

"Okay."

"Where is it?"

"Uh... I don't really know. It's not along the trail. I found it both times by accident."

"*Both* times?"

"Yeah. I stumbled across it earlier this week."

"But you don't know where it is in relation to the trail."

Tara shook her head.

"Okay...well, I've got the walkie-talkie in a bag of rice. We can try it out tomorrow sometime. What are we doing for dinner tonight now that it's just you and me?"

"I don't know. I'm not very hungry, to be honest."

Her father nodded and touched a hand to his stomach. "Yeah, I'm not either."

"So, I guess we'll just snack whenever."

"Works for me, I guess. Hey, did you want to watch a movie later?"

"Sure. Let me know when you're done in here."

Once upstairs, she locked her bedroom door behind her and crawled into bed to read a book. Thoughts of Belle crashed over one another in her head, though, making the pit of her stomach warm with anticipation. She was too distracted to read, so she tossed her novel aside and grabbed a sketchpad from inside her nightstand instead. Like her father, Tara enjoyed drawing, though she was nowhere near as good as her father was at her age. She'd only started teaching herself a few months earlier, with the help of books from her school library.

Before long, she was drawing Belle submerged in the plunge pool of the waterfall with her portable CD player beside her.

Something was wrong. That's all she knew when she opened her eyes in the middle of the night, hours after watching a movie with her father.

She was itchy. And tickled. How was she being tickled?

As she blinked and sat up in the darkness, she fumbled for the lamp switch beside her. When the room illuminated a second later, she began to scream. Her bed and body were covered in tiny spiders. There had to be dozens of them, maybe even hundreds.

Her father bounded up the stairs and threw open her door a moment later. "What? What is it?"

Then he saw the spiders.

Tara jumped out of bed and began knocking as many off her as she could. Her father joined in, swiping them off her and smashing as many of them under his slippers as he could. Tara continued to cry and scream, shaking in terror. Her father swiped and smacked at her, before saying, "Just get in the shower! Quick! Wash them off if there are any in your hair or somewhere."

Tara ran into the hall to the bathroom, slamming the door shut behind her. Arnold remained in her bedroom, hunting the spiders that remained. He couldn't believe how many of them he'd killed already. There must have been a nest in the room, freshly hatched. He wondered if the spiders were poisonous or not, and decided he should catch one alive to show someone just in case.

While he did that in the bedroom, Tara savagely scraped at herself in the shower, overflowing her hands with shampoo to run through her hair in hope that the chemicals would kill any spiders hiding there. Several fell into the drain during her stay, dead or dying. She didn't know how she could ever leave the bathroom feeling clean. She was twitching all over, as if the bastards were still on her. At last, she closed the drain and allowed the tub to fill. She then filled it with body wash and dunked her head under water until she was numb, and scratched at her scalp with her fingernails.

More than thirty minutes had passed before she got out of the tub to dry off. When she did emerge from the bathroom, trembling in shock and disgust, her father emerged from her bedroom to tell her what he'd done.

"I caught one to make sure it isn't poisonous," he said. "And killed the rest. I think you have a nest in there or something. Those spiders were hatchlings. Maybe they aren't poisonous that young. I don't know. But I'll find out." He paused and looked back over his shoulder at the room before continuing. "I think it's best if you don't sleep in there tonight. I cleaned up their guts as best as I could, and sprayed the hell out of the room with that poison your mother keeps in the closet. Hell, that might be reason enough not to sleep there overnight, because it might not be the best stuff to be breathing."

"I'm not going anywhere near the fucking room tonight," Tara said, forgetting to censor herself.

Instead of getting on Tara about it, her father said, "I wouldn't if I were you. I'll try to figure out a better way to clean it out tomorrow. Maybe call over an exterminator while I'm at it. We don't need any more nests in this place."

Tara nodded and shivered within the towel wrapped around her.

"You think you got them all off you?" her father asked.

Tara shook harder in response. "Please, just stop talking about them."

"Sorry. You can sleep on the couch in the living room. Have a sleepover with the TV or whatever."

"Thanks."

Her father turned away from her and headed toward his own room. Tara considered grabbing clothes from her dresser, but thought better of it. Right now, she wanted that room to burn, along with everything inside it. So, she headed downstairs with the towel and found clothing in the laundry room to wear.

In the morning, Tara forced herself to drink a cup of coffee. She hadn't slept for more than a few minutes at a time after the spider incident. Every time she drifted into dreams, spiders would invade them, hungry for her eyes. She was exhausted.

As she hovered by the sink with her mug of coffee, she felt the uneasy suspicion that someone was watching her. She looked around the room, assuming it was her father. But the downstairs level was empty and quiet.

She turned to the window and looked outside. There at the treeline was the same young woman she'd spotted several nights earlier in the rain, only this time she wasn't naked. Instead, she wore a crimson cloak and hood.

"What the fuck?" Tara mumbled, lowering her coffee and leaning over the sink for a closer look.

The girl met her gaze before turning away and disappearing into the woods.

Tara raced into the laundry room to find a pair of socks and dry shoes to wear. Once she had them on, she hurried outside and looked for the girl's tracks in the damp soil. Though there were some at the treeline, they were impossible to see through the woods. Leaves littered the ground, as did puddles of water and mud. Tara wasn't a tracker by any means, and lost her way after a few seconds.

"Damn it!"

She wanted to keep looking, but thought of her father waking up to find her missing. So, she returned to the house, wrote him a note saying she was taking a morning walk, and grabbed the walkie-talkie he had drying out in a bag of rice. She didn't know if it worked, but she hardly cared either way. She was bringing it mostly for show.

Back in the woods, she entered the trees from where she'd spotted the girl and continued straight. She hoped her spy hadn't taken a winding path to the house.

In an unusual amount of time, she stepped out of the trees and onto the rock surrounding the waterfall and its pool. Confused, Tara looked back over her shoulder and wondered how long she'd been walking. It seemed like she'd only left the yard a minute ago. The waterfall shouldn't have been this close at all. It made no sense geographically either. The mountain didn't rise this close to her house.

"What is going on?" she asked herself aloud.

"Sorry, I did that."

Tara startled and turned toward the waterfall. Sitting beside it with a small fire at her feet was the cloaked woman. She had a skillet of sizzling eggs held over the fire, and her hood was now pulled back to reveal her tempting red hair. She looked up at Tara and smiled.

"You hungry?" she asked.

Tara took several steps in her direction. "Who are you?"

"My name is Ardere."

"Ardere?"

The girl nodded and moved her gaze back onto the eggs. She shuffled the skillet over the fire a moment longer before pulling them back to rest atop the rocks surrounding her.

"Why are you out here?" Tara asked, studying her.

"I've been out here for a month or so," the girl told her. "I hadn't realized a new family had moved into the house."

"Did you used to…squat there or something?"

The girl laughed and shook her head. "No. I have kept my distance for the most part."

"Why were you watching me the other night?"

"That's not the only time I've watched you." The girl turned to produce a stone plate from behind her, and shook the eggs out of the skillet onto it. "Here," she said, holding out the plate to Tara.

"No, that's okay."

"Suit yourself." The girl began to eat with her hands, making a mess.

"Are you homeless?" Tara asked, not sure how to better word the question.

"I suppose you might consider me homeless," the girl replied. "But I don't think of myself that way."

"Why are you out here then?"

"I live in the woods all over. I'll stay in a place for a while, then leave. I've been on a mission for years and years, but finally things are lining up."

"What things?"

"People, mostly. My girls are on a pilgrimage as we speak. But we could certainly use another helpful hand."

Tara was confused and said as much.

"There's much to learn," the girl continued. "But I don't just freely offer such knowledge."

Tara opened her mouth but found that she didn't know what she could say to Ardere that wouldn't sound offensive.

The girl finished her eggs, cleaned her lips, chin, and hands in the pool, then stood. Water glistened around her mouth, and Tara sensed a strange arousal bubbling inside her.

"Follow me," the girl told her, turning toward the waterfall.

Tara did as she was told, though she didn't understand why. Something about Ardere was luring her away from safety, she felt, but she couldn't stop herself. She felt propelled—no, *compelled*, to follow the girl and see whatever it was she wanted to show Tara.

They entered the cave from the right, hugging the wall to avoid getting soaked by the waterfall. Inside, several candles had been placed along the walls to light the space. Tara observed the drawings she'd seen before, and noticed they'd multiplied in scale—there were more eyes now and more people worshiping from the woods beneath them.

"What is all this?" she asked the girl. "I've found eyes carved into trees also."

The girl turned to face her, several feet between them.

This close, Tara couldn't help but lust after Ardere's beauty. What was this unnatural possession she felt washing over her? It was as if the girl herself was intoxicating and…magic? That couldn't be it, but Tara thought the word nevertheless.

"The Eye of Eyes is my King. The Higher Power. These eyes in the sky you see here are His watchmen, you could say."

"I have no idea what you're talking about," Tara admitted.

"Join me and I can teach you everything."

"Join you?"

"As I've said, the Others are on a pilgrimage at this time, but I can bring you up to speed while they're away."

The girl held out a hand for Tara to take. It was scarred all over, as if it had been cut many times. Uneasy, Tara looked at it. She then felt an energy surge down her arm, attempting to lift it. Scared of the feeling, Tara took two steps back from the woman and shook her head. "What the hell is going on? I feel…st–strange."

Ardere smiled in a way that made Tara shiver. As she lowered her hand, she said, "Have you seen any of the eyes yet?"

Tara thought of her waking nightmare from two nights earlier, the one with the fiery eyeball that launched itself down her throat. "N–no," she lied.

The girl's eyes narrowed, but for less than a second.

"I, uh, have to go," Tara said, moving toward the exit. "My father is going to wonder where I am."

"Isn't that why you brought that device on your belt?" the girl asked.

Tara looked down at the walkie-talkie, having completely forgotten about it. "Yes, but it isn't working," she said.

The girl nodded, watching her.

As Tara turned away and hurried outside, she heard Ardere say, "Thank you for letting me use your bathroom the other night."

She didn't tell her father. How could she?

She spent the rest of the morning in the living room on the couch, drawing and reading. More than once, she lost herself in a trance, only to find herself sketching eyes and Ardere all over her pad. Scared by this new, obsessive development, she tore out the pages and crumpled them into balls at the foot of the couch to be thrown away later. Who the hell was that girl? And what mission was she referring to? She said years had gone by, but she looked to be in her early twenties, if even in her twenties. It didn't make sense. She must have grown up in a cult or something. Maybe she was one of those crazy mountain people you read about in horror stories.

And yet, she was beautiful, a hypnotic attractiveness.

Tara cursed herself for thinking such things and decided to check in on her father. He was in his office painting as usual.

"What's up, kiddo?" he asked as she stepped inside.

"I don't know. Just bored, I guess."

"I have an exterminator coming this afternoon," he told her.

"That's good."

"You haven't seen any more of the damn things, have you?"

She shook her head.

"Good, good. Why don't you take your bike into town for a while?"

"Yeah, maybe."

Her father's gaze narrowed. "Is everything okay?"

"Yeah. Just…bored."

He didn't believe her, but nodded anyway. "Let me know if you need any money to get lunch or anything," he said, turning back to his painting.

"Okay, thanks."

Tara left the office, not sure where to go. Did she have the energy or interest to bike into town? She didn't think so. Not alone, at least. She was tempted to call Belle, even if it was to just talk for a minute and nothing more, but restrained herself from picking up the phone. She didn't know much about Belle's parents and didn't want to annoy them by calling. She'd dealt with some rude parents in the past, and therefore never made the first move to call someone as a result.

Veni ad me…

Tara nearly jumped out of her skin. She looked around herself to find who was talking, but there was no one there. Her father was the only other person home, and he was still in his office. Not only that, his voice wasn't soft or pleasant like the one she'd just heard. Whoever had spoken had a voice that was both feminine and…

Enchanting?

Veni ad me…

There it was again. Was Tara hearing it from inside her head? She searched the house for anyone else, but there was only her father in his office. Whenever she walked by, he would turn and wait for her to enter. But she never did. If he was curious about her pacing, he kept it to himself by returning to his work.

Tara determined the voice was without a body. She didn't understand how that could be, but the past week had been strange in other ways, as well. The nightmares, the spiders, the muddy footprints that vanished on their own...

And Ardere. The girl in the woods living in a secret cave behind a waterfall that seemed to change locations as it pleased.

"I'm losing my fucking mind," Tara told herself, heading outside to clear her head. But before she could enter the woods and find her trail, she stopped herself to reconsider.

If Ardere was out there, they might run into each other again. And Tara wasn't ready for that. Not just yet.

So, she went to the shed to fetch her bicycle.

I guess I'm going into town, after all, she decided.

Saturday night was even worse than the Night of Spiders, as she'd come to think of it. The voice in her head had started talking more and more throughout the day, to the point that it was somehow overlapping itself. There were more phrases than before, all of them Latin or Italian—she wasn't sure which, and also wasn't sure how much they even differed. But she'd recognized a few words over the course of the day, including *exitium*, which translated to "destruction". Even without understanding the rest, she began to worry.

The voice wasn't the only difficult part of her night. She was also having regular hallucinations. There were eyes on her all the time, peering at her around corners and in reflections. Even in the darkness, they would blink and stare. Whenever she neared sleep, she'd feel vines wrapping around her ankles, eager to drag her out the window and to the woods. She fought these hallucinations and screamed so often that her father suggested they go to the hospital to figure out what was wrong.

"You must have a dangerous fever," he told her, "for you to be seeing and hearing things that aren't here. I'm really worried, Tara! We should go. Please."

But she fought him to stay home without being able to explain why. Maybe she worried somehow would call her possessed and order an exorcist. Or perhaps worse, someone would deem her mentally unstable and put her in an asylum.

It took several sleeping pills to put her to sleep, and by then it was after 3 a.m.

It was nearing noon on Sunday when Arnold Wilkins shook his daughter awake.

"Wha…what is it?" she slurred, blinking against the light breaking through her curtains.

"The phone rang for you, sweetie. It was Belle," he told her.

Tara sat up and clapped her cheeks to wake up. "Right now? She's on the phone?"

"Not anymore. I spoke with her, though."

"What did she say?"

"First things first," her father said, watching her with a furrowed brow. "How are you feeling?"

Tara considered this by scanning the room for anything that didn't belong. Everything appeared normal enough, and there were no voices speaking Latin inside her head.

"I feel…fine," she said with a shrug and smile. "Really."

Her father placed the back of his hand against her forehead, then felt the back of her neck. "You're not hot," he said.

"What did Belle want?" Tara asked again, eager for good news to help save the weekend for her.

"I'm not sure. I told her you were sleeping in late, and she asked for you to call her back."

Tara threw back the covers and climbed out of bed. "I'll call her back now!"

"Wait, wait," her father said, taking her by the shoulders. "Are you *sure* you're okay? Last night was kind of scary. You really freaked me out."

"I feel fine, Dad. Really."

"Have you, uh, noticed any spider bites on you since that night?"

She shook her head. "No, why?"

"I thought maybe yesterday's craziness could be a reaction to a bite."

"I haven't noticed anything," she said, "but that does make me wonder. I'll take a thorough look in the shower."

"Good. Okay. Go call your friend back."

Tara hurried downstairs and into the kitchen. She wasted no time dialing Belle and cradling the phone tight to her ear. When an unfamiliar man answered the call, she began to panic, her anxiety getting the best of her. "Oh, uh, hi. This is, uh, Tara. From school. Is Belle there?"

"Yeah. Just a minute," the voice said. The phone was set down on something hard with a clicking sound.

Tara waited by pacing about the kitchen and wrapping the phone cord around her midsection as she turned in circles until she was dizzy.

"Hello?"

"Belle?"

"Tara?

"Yes!"

Belle laughed. "You sound alert. I guess sleeping in until lunch does you good."

"I had a rough night. It was close to four before I even got to sleep, I think."

"Oh, that sucks."

"Dad said you called for me."

"Well, I certainly didn't call for him."

"I don't blame you."

Both girls giggled.

"I was wondering if you wanted to get lunch," Belle said. "I'm feeling much better now."

"Yes! Yes, yes, yes."

"Great. How about Ryan's? Do you know where that is?"

"The burger joint by the bookstore?"

"That's the one."

"Sure. What time?"

"I'm getting hungry now if you're available," she said, smiling through her voice.

"Uh, let me see… I can be there in like forty-five minutes. I need to shower and get dressed and bike over there. Is that okay?"

"Yeah, that works. I'll see you there!"

"Okay!"

Tara hung up the phone and hurried up to the bathroom, almost knocking her father over as she passed him on the stairs.

"Woah, what's going on?" he called after her.

"I'm going to meet Belle for lunch."

"Be safe!" he yelled from downstairs as she undressed next to the shower.

Though Tara was in a hurry, she checked herself for bites as best she could before getting under the spray of hot water. She found nothing but considered the validity of her father's hypothesis. Maybe she was having a reaction. The bite could be located somewhere on her scalp, beneath her hair. Or even in an awkward location along her back. She figured a bite should itch but they didn't even know what kind of spider had hatched in her bedroom. Her father had shown the exterminator the one he'd captured, but the guy didn't recognize it.

After her shower, Tara toweled off fast and got dressed. She tortured herself in the mirror before forcing herself outside to the shed—she no longer had time to continue fucking around with her looks. Belle was waiting.

She rode fast into town, working her legs harder than she had since running track for her previous high school. Her calves and thighs were burning by the time she reached Ryan's at 12:30. She found Belle already inside, sitting in a booth facing the entrance. She almost jumped out of her seat when Tara stepped inside.

271

She's just as happy to see you, Tara told herself. *This is good. She must like you, too.*

"Hey, Belle," she said on approach, a shy brush of the hair behind her ear.

"It feels like it's been ages," her friend said, hugging her.

Tara felt the pit of her stomach warm and her breath hitch in her chest. "It does."

Belle pulled away and said, "Well, I guess we should order something and then we can sit."

"Oh, right. Duh."

They headed to the counter and placed their order. When Belle tried paying, Belle pushed her hand away and handled it instead. As they waited at the corner of the counter for their food, Tara asked Belle how she was feeling.

"I'm still a little run down, but my throat is only a little scratchy. I should be at school tomorrow. I can't keep missing."

"Well, I think I might have scared off Kia, at least."

"Really? What happened?"

"Thursday, she hit me when we got off the bus and—"

"Wait, what? She *hit* you?"

"Yeah, but I was like *possessed* or something, like totally pissed when she did. I snapped and told her I'd tear her apart if she did it again."

Belle's eyes widened. "Whaaaaa… Really?"

"Yeah. I think I also called her a cunt."

"*Holy shit.*"

Their food arrived at the counter then. They took the trays over to a booth and sat down—Belle was eager to hear more about the Kia confrontation.

"What did she do after you said all that?"

"She looked shocked. I hurried home but…I felt *good*."

"And Friday?"

"She avoided me. And during the walk home, I even yelled at her to keep walking or something."

"None of this sounds like you."

"Because it's not! Seriously, I have no idea what was coming over me. Both times, I felt this crazy energy swelling up inside me. I'm lucky I didn't jump on her back and start pulling out her hair or something."

"Damn, girl. Good to know you're on my side," Belle said, laughing.

Tara straightened as she took a drink from her soda, and contemplated telling Belle what else had been going on with her and the girl in the woods. She was going back and forth with herself on the subject—just as she had during the bike ride into town—when Belle took notice of her change.

"What's wrong? You've tensed up."

Tara smiled at her, pleased that Belle could see through her so easily. It made her feel truly noticed by her friend that she wanted more from down the road.

"There's been more going on," she admitted.

"Like what? I only missed two days!"

273

"Not with school. Outside of school."

"Oh. Is everything alright?"

Tara looked away from Belle as she thought things through. "I've been seeing and hearing things this weekend."

"Like what?"

"Someone speaking Latin in my head. And…there was the night I woke up covered in a hundred baby spiders."

"Wait, *what*?" Belle squirmed in her seat, dropping her burger onto the tray. "Spiders?"

"Yeah. And I didn't imagine them like some of the other stuff. My dad had to come rescue me. A nest had hatched or something in my room."

"Holy shit…"

"Yeah, I nearly passed out from it."

"What else have you seen?"

"Crazy things… Like eyes. Everywhere."

"Disembodied?"

"Yeah. And it all started after I found this cave in the woods."

"What cave?"

"It's behind this waterfall behind my house. But I don't know the location exactly. It always seems to change."

Belle eyed her in a way that made Tara uncomfortable. Was she losing her? She didn't want to scare Belle away from her.

274

"Forget it," she said. "It's crazy, I know. I think... um... I think it's just my waking nightmares returning. I had them a lot as a toddler, my parents have told me."

"What's that?"

"I guess it's like sleepwalking. I'd be awake and moving around, talking, eyes open. But I'd be dreaming and unable to see or hear my parents as they tried to calm me down."

"Jesus."

"They said I did it for like two years. I woke them up a lot during that time."

For a minute, they ate in silence before moving onto other conversations. Their lunch stretched on for an hour before Belle told her she wanted to see the waterfall. Though Tara was a little worried they'd run into Ardere there—assuming the girl was real and not one of her hallucinations—but then Belle shocked her by leaning across the table and kissing her on the lips. Though it was quick, there was a force to it that suggested physical interest in more. Tara's mouth hung open after as she stared at Belle, wondering whether or not she'd imagine the kiss.

"Did you just—"

Belle nodded, her cheeks blooming red.

Tara swallowed and nodded back. "Okay. Let's go to my house."

Belle jumped out of the booth as Tara quickly threw their trash together on one tray. "Right behind you!"

They biked side by side as often as they could. The town was small and pretty quiet, so they were able to spread out on the road multiple times during the ride. When they reached Tara's house fifteen minutes later, they jumped off their bikes and allowed them to crash into one another along the side of the driveway.

"So, this is it," Tara said, a little out of breath.

"Cute. I love that you're surrounded by the woods. Nice and private."

"I need the woods nearby," Tara admitted. "It's how I reset."

"What do you mean?"

"When I'm overwhelmed by things or upset, going into nature really helps me get my head back on straight."

"Oh, I get that. My parents and I used to hike a lot together. But now we're not around each other all that much anymore."

"Before we do anything, I think I should introduce you to my dad," Tara said, heading toward the house. "He'd be pissed if I didn't."

"What about your mom?"

"She's away for a couple days for work."

Tara led her inside and called for her father, though she assumed he was in the office as usual. He replied from down the hall, and they followed his voice. When they stepped into his office space, they found him painting a dark forest across a large canvas, the biggest Tara had seen him use in months.

"Oh, we have company," he said, smiling upon seeing Belle hiding behind Tara in the doorway. "You must be Belle."

She nodded shyly. "Hello."

"This is my dad, Arnold," Tara said.

"You can call me *Mr. Wilkins*," her father told Belle, dropping his smile. But a second later, he grinned again, laughing. "Nah, I'm just kidding. Arnold is fine."

"We're going to hang out for a bit," Tara told him. "Probably go out to the woods for a walk."

"Take the radio. I still don't know if it works, though. Test it out for me and let me know if I need to replace it already."

Tara agreed and led Belle into the kitchen to find the rice bag with the walkie-talkie inside it. When she took it out, she switched it on. The speaker crackled in response. "I guess it's working," she said to Belle with a shrug as she clipped it to the side of her belt.

They returned outside after getting drinks of water, and headed toward the woods.

"How far does this go?" Belle asked her.

"No idea. At least a few miles, I think. We're at the base of a mountain."

"Have you carved out any trails yet?"

"The previous owners made several."

"Are we going to the waterfall?"

"If I can find it."

Belle bumped into her for second. Tara wasn't sure if it was an accident or not, but she blushed nonetheless.

"You don't know where it is?" Belle asked.

"No, that's part of the strange stuff that's been happening..."

"What do you mean?"

"It seems to change locations in the woods," Tara explained. "I know that sounds crazy, but I always stumble upon it by accident, and one of the times it was only shortly after entering the woods. Which makes no sense because it was much further out the other two times."

"Are you sure it was the same waterfall each time?"

"Yeah. The cave was there every time."

"And what makes the cave so special?"

"Um..."

Belle gave her a sideways look as they walked through the trees. "What is it?"

"The cave is full of drawings."

"Ooo, like ancient stuff?"

"No. There's a...um... A girl lives out here."

Belle stopped. Tara walked several more steps before pausing to turn around.

"A girl is living out here?" Belle asked her.

"That's what she told me."

"Like, camping?"

"In the cave, I guess."

"Oh, that is so fucking weird."

Tara nodded.

"So, you've met her? Is she crazy? Dangerous?"

"I don't know. She said some strange stuff to me, but she didn't *act* crazy."

Belle bridged the gap between them and they started walking once more. "Well...okay. Let's find this waterfall."

They searched for an hour before giving up. As they left the woods and headed back toward the house, Belle asked, "Is it possible the waterfall was another hallucination?"

"I guess so," Tara mumbled. She was angry and embarrassed.

As if sensing this, Belle took her hand and squeezed it as they approached their discarded bikes. "It's okay," Belle said. "Maybe your dad was onto something about the spider bite. You think you'll go to the doctor? Maybe have them draw blood or something?"

"I don't know. Maybe." She felt shut down, and in front of Belle, no less. Tara wanted to scurry under her bed covers and hide.

Belle bent over to pick up her bike. "I'll see you at school tomorrow?"

Tara nodded.

Belle positioned herself close to Tara and said, "I enjoyed getting some time with you," she said. "You know, outside of school."

With a weak smile, Tara kept her gaze to the side, scared to meet Belle's eyes. But Belle was far more assertive than she, and placed a hand against Tara's cheek to turn her face. Tara swallowed as her heart began to race.

"Hey," Belle said.

Tara met her gaze.

Belle leaned in and kissed her deeply. Tara felt like she was on fire and levitating. When Belle pulled away slowly, Tara's eyes were still shut, her mouth still open a little.

"See you tomorrow," Belle said, climbing onto her bike and taking off down the driveway.

Tara watched her go, breathless for several minutes. Once she'd collected herself enough to walk, she headed into the house to find her father. When she entered his office to tell him Belle had gone home, she almost fell backwards in shock.

His painting on the large canvas now featured a dozen eyes of various sizes littering the night sky. Tara tried to scream but it caught in her throat as she stumbled against the doorway. Her father turned in his chair to look at her and said, "What's wrong?"

"Wh—"

"You don't like it?"

Tara squeezed her eyes shut, counted to three with slow breaths, and then looked at the painting again. The eyes were no longer there.

"Thank god," she whispered.

Her father watched her close, concerned. "What's going on, sweetie? Are you hallucinating again?"

She licked her lips and shrugged. "I'm b—better now."

He nodded, his eyes glued to her face. "Why don't you send Belle home and get some rest?"

"She actually just left."

"That's probably for the best. Take some, I don't know, allergy medicine or something and lie down for a bit. I know you've only been up a couple hours, but you're really making me worry."

"Belle said I should get blood drawn. To test your spider bite theory," Tara offered, still trying to calm herself. The tremors in her fingers were still ringing.

"That might not be such a bad idea. I'll call the doctor in the morning and see what we can set up."

"What about school?"

"I can take you out for an hour," he told her. "And if they raise a fuss, they can fuck themselves."

Tara smiled and turned away from her father. "I guess I'll go lie down then."

"Good."

Once upstairs in her room, she climbed under her blankets and embraced the darkness beneath them. Her heart began to steady in rhythm a few minutes later. Tara smiled to herself and relaxed atop the bed, curling onto her side and getting comfortable. She was almost asleep when she felt something watching her. She opened her eyes slowly and saw only darkness.

At first.

Then an eye blinked back at her in the black.

Monday morning, Tara looked a mess. After going to bed Sunday afternoon, she'd struggled with waking nightmares and hallucinations all through the day and night. Her eyes were red from rubbing them and her hair was in knots. She didn't even try to make herself presentable for school—she was just too tired and haunted to care.

When Belle saw her in between classes, she asked what was going on.

"It got so much worse after seeing you yesterday." Tara yawned as she fumbled with her books at her locker.

"How so?"

"I couldn't get any sleep without a nightmare. I just kept seeing things and… I don't even know if this conversation is actually happening or not. I'm in a daze."

"Jesus, Tara. Maybe you should go home."

"My dad is supposed to get me at some point to take me to the doctor, like you suggested."

"Good. Just hang in there until it arrives. Take it easy."

"I'm trying."

Later, in her fourth class, Tara hit a wall. Her teacher had given a stack of assignments to the front row to pass around the class. When it came time for Tara to pick a paper and pass it along, her head was down on the desk and she was oblivious. The student passing her the stack—a guy from the wrestling team—saw this and dropped the papers onto her head. As they scattered, she looked up, zeroed in on him and his laughing friends, and screamed for him to "Fuck the hell off." The teacher kicked her out of class to go see the principal.

But she didn't go to the office. Instead, she walked right out the front doors, through the parking lot, and to the road. She intended on walking home regardless of the consequences. As for her father picking her up, she'd forgotten—she wasn't even aware of the world around her at this point. Every time she directed her gaze to anything specific, she would see an eye where it didn't belong. The Stop signs blinked at her, as did the trees and the hoods of passing cars. She couldn't escape them. She was being watched no matter where she turned.

Iungere nobis...

...aut pascere caelum.

"Shut up," she groaned, clapping her hands over her ears as she stumbled down the road. "Shut up, shut up, shut up."

It felt like her brain was on fire. On occasion, a wave of heat would wash over her entire body, making her sick. She shook and twitched and lacked control of herself. It was as if she was moving on autopilot.

Time had also changed for her. It seemed she was leaping forward every time she blinked or lifted her head to inspect her surroundings. She soon found herself in the woods behind her house, though she should have still been several miles away. When she looked down at herself, she saw her legs were trembling. They ached. The soles of her feet were blistered and stinging. The back of her neck and arms were red with sunburn.

"How did I get here?" she asked herself. *This doesn't make any sense.*

"Well, look at you."

Tara blinked again and looked up from her shuffling feet. She was stepping onto the rocks surrounding the water-fall. Ardere was standing by the pool, watching her.

"You," Tara said, sleepy.

"Me. I have to say, Tara—you don't look so good."

"What do you want, Ardere?"

"Oh, good. You remember my name. Effects can vary with this spell, I'll admit. Some girls completely lose their fucking minds." The girl laughed and approached Tara, removing her cloak as she neared. "Have you reconsidered my offer? The girls will be back any day now. I'm sure they'd love a new recruit."

"I don't understand," Tara told her. "I don't understand what is going on. Who you are. What you want."

"The Eye of Eyes provides. We are preparing for the end of the world, I suppose you could say. Only it won't be the end for us. Far from it."

Tara was standing still but wavering back and forth as if she might fall any second. "You're crazy."

"Let me try something else," the girl said, producing an ancient knife from her cloak and splitting open the palm of her hand. Before Tara could even think to act, the girl placed her bloodied palm against Tara's chest and whispered something in an unfamiliar language. It could have been Latin or something even older.

"What are you doing?" Tara asked. Suddenly, she was flooded with images she couldn't explain. Marching trees. A blackened sky filled with eyes. Raging fires. Blood and gore. A monstrous creature that stood tall and white. Then galaxies of stars and planets bursting like bombs, one by one until an all-consuming, blinding light struck Tara so hard that she was thrown backwards onto the rocks.

"How about now?" Ardere asked, standing over. "Do you believe me now?"

Scared, Tara picked herself up from the ground and ran into the woods, away from the waterfall.

Ardere called after her in a sing-songy voice, "If you do not choose us, that nasty fever in your brain will only get worse."

Spilling out of the trees, Tara ran into her backyard. She scrambled across the grass, tripping over her feet a few times before reaching the back door and trying to open it. But it was locked and she didn't have any of her things with her. She must have left it all at school in the classroom.

"Shit!"

She began to pound on the door, unaware that her father had left to pick her up from school. She couldn't take it anymore—her brain was burning and the voices were so constant and overlapping that she couldn't understand a word of them anymore. She began to shoulder the door harder and harder until the lock broke and she fell inside. Kicking the door shut behind her, she crawled into the kitchen crying.

She lifted herself up against the island counter and found herself a knife.

She needed to make the voices stop.

Arnold Wilkins was furious. Not only did the school tell him Tara had dismissed herself without a word to anyone, but she'd first screamed obscenities during class. How could she have left on foot, though? He knew she wasn't doing well, but this was taking things to another level. She was becoming violent and self-destructive. He needed to get her tested straight away, and not at the doctor's office. He needed to take her to a hospital and hope for the best.

As he drove home, he called his wife to tell her what had been happening. She said she'd be home tomorrow afternoon—it was the best she could do. Frustrated, Arnold ended the call without saying goodbye. When he pulled into the driveway, he raced down it toward the house, kicking up rocks along the way.

"Tara!" he yelled, storming into the house with his keys in hand. "Where are you?"

It didn't take long to find her. There was blood all over the kitchen floor, in circles as if Tara had been pacing. When he saw her standing over the sink with her hands held under the running faucet, he felt his heart leap into his throat.

"Tara?"

She didn't turn. Her back remained on him as he inched closer.

"Tara? Honey?"

Still nothing.

There was blood on her shoulders and arms, but he couldn't see her hands. She appeared to be washing them. Where was the blood coming from? What had she done to herself? He needed to call for an ambulance. But first, he needed to know where she was hurt…

"Tara?" He placed a hand on her shoulder and turned her.

His daughter spun in place and thrust a bloodied knife into his gut, pushing him back against the island. Now that he could see her face, he realized why she hadn't heard him—her ears were gone. Crimson threads of skin hung in their place, entwined with her sticky hair.

He couldn't feel the knife at first. But upon seeing his daughter's self-mutilation, the blade in his gut made Arnold lower his gaze and scream.

"What have you done?"

At first, it didn't seem that Tara recognized them. But then her eyes widened in shock and she stumbled backwards against the sink.

"Da–daddy?"

Arnold repeated himself as he fell to the floor, clutching the knife handle protruding from him. "What have you done?"

Tara began to sob, turning her head erratically from side to side as she looked elsewhere. Arnold watched her, confused. It seemed as if she could see things that he could not.

She began screaming at the kitchen behind him, though there was nothing there he could see or hear.

"Leave him alone! Stay away from us! Stay away!"

Arnold shuddered as a cold swept over him. "Honey? Wha–what's happening? Who's here? Call 911, please…"

Tara's eyes fell on him and narrowed. Again, she didn't seem to recognize him. She took hold of the knife handle and tore the blade out of his gut. He pressed his hands against his wound as the knife came out, and fell onto his side, gasping and crying from the pain. Tara stood over him, a girl possessed. Her eyes had whitened, as if she'd gone blind.

Arnold began to plead with her as his energy ebbed from his body. "Honey, please… Call for help…"

The knife flashed through the air and planted into the side of his neck this time. He grunted, but little else. The knife stabbed into him again and again until Arnold couldn't feel anything anymore. With his face pressed against the bloodied tiled floor, he looked toward the fridge and faded into nothingness.

Two days passed. Belle had not seen Tara in school, nor had she been able to reach her by telephone. She was sick with worry. Something must have happened.

When she arrived outside Tara's house Wednesday evening, just as the sun was setting over the surrounding trees, she saw two vehicles in the driveway, both crooked as if they'd parked in a hurry.

They're home, she told herself as she leaned her bicycle against a tree. *That has to be a good thing, right?*

She sniffed the air. Something was burning in the backyard. She could see smoke in the air and smell meat. Were they having a cookout for dinner?

Belle's concern began to fade. The Wilkins family must have been celebrating Tara's recovery. Maybe they'd taken her to the hospital after all.

She rounded the vehicles and headed down the side yard to the back of the house. When she turned the corner, she found a bonfire burning with a slight crackle, its flames low and perhaps dying. In the midst of the charred wood pile were two shapes that made her freeze mid-step.

What?

She couldn't process what she was seeing. Those were bodies, weren't they? Blackened, flaking bodies with exposed skulls and jaws hanging open.

"No," Belle said aloud to herself, as if that would erase the scene before her. "No. No."

Something crashed from inside the house. Belle turned, but did not move any further into the yard. She was frozen in place, terrified.

Someone had murdered the Wilkins. Was Tara dead, too? Was the killer still inside the house, robbing them?

Before she could force herself to turn away from the house and run, the back door opened, its frame splintered around the lock. Tara stepped outside with a revolver in hand, her eyes lowered upon it. She walked several steps outside before looking up and spotting Belle at the corner, eyes wide and tears staining her cheeks.

"Belle?"

"Ta–Tara?"

For several long seconds, nobody said a word. As Belle watched Tara from afar, she realized her friend's ears were missing and that she was wearing the same clothes she'd had on Monday morning, the last she'd seen her. Only now, they were stained with blood and dirt.

"What happened to you?" Belle asked, her voice barely a whisper. Did it even matter, though? Her friend could no longer hear anything.

Tara's face crumpled upon itself and she began to sob. "I can't make it stop," she screamed, gripping the revolver tight in her hands. Her words were muffled and unclear. "They won't leave me alone! I can still hear them! I can still see them!"

Belle watched in horror as her friend paced back and forth about the backyard with her gun, tears soaking her face as she stomped her right feet.

"It must stop!"

Belle swallowed and looked toward the open door. If she could run inside and find the telephone, call the police...

Would Tara shoot her? Had Tara been the one to kill her parents?

"Why are you here?!" Tara screamed, looking at Belle now with mistrust. "You're another trick! Another fucking trick!"

Belle wanted to run—was desperate to get out of there—but her muscles were locked in place. Fear had a death grip on her and would not let go.

Tara fell to her knees and smacked her hands and the revolver against her head, where her ears used to be. "They won't shut up! That fucking girl in the woods—she did this to me! She did this to me!"

Belle looked toward the trees, felt the sudden weight of someone's gaze upon her. But there was no one else there but Tara.

"Let's... Let's get you to a hos–hospital," Belle offered, holding out a shaking hand toward her friend. "We–we can fix this. We can get you help."

Tara's eyes shot back on her. "No more tricks!" she screamed, raising the revolver and taking aim at Belle.

Finally, she found it in herself to run. Turning, she fell, and got back onto her feet. A blast of gunfire echoed around her as Tara pulled the trigger on her revolver. Belle did not stop. She made it to her bike a second later and jumped onto it. As she began to pedal down the driveway, she looked back over her shoulder.

There was someone wearing a crimson cloak stepping out of the woods toward Tara as she stumbled into the side yard with her gun still raised. Tara turned to face her, screamed, and thrust the revolver against her temple. When the dull shot echoed, Belle lost control of her bike and fell, unable to remove her eyes from Tara's collapsing form.

From the gravel, bruised and bleeding, Belle watched as the cloaked figure turned away from Tara to look in her direction instead.

The figure lowered their hood and smiled.

Veni ad me...

293

Acknowledgments

First, I would like to thank Slashic Horror Press. The journey in taking this book to publication wasn't what I would call easygoing. In the past year, I went through an identity crisis and autistic burnout, both of which left me creatively disabled and emotionally broken. Luckily for me, the great guys at Slashic Horror Press somehow found it in their hearts to be forgiving and flexible with me the whole time, despite how much I must have frustrated them with my indecisive and depressed nature. Not only did they keep me around, they were professional and focused the entire time. Without them, this book wouldn't exist. Giving these guys a manuscript I could be proud of propelled me to write a ton of new content to replace what we originally had in place, so literally, this book would not have existed in this form whatsoever without them.

To David-Jack for the awesome editing he did on these stories. They are worlds better now thanks to his attention and recommendations.

To Leeroy for the support and promotions of my work online. Social media can be hell, so it's good we have him to cover it.

To Rosco for another great cover. I've worked with him a few times over the years, and he always does an awesome job.

To all the readers who have supported me. Every share and review makes me feel special, even the negative ones. There's a lot out there to read, so having someone give me a chance is an amazing feeling.

To the authors and creators that were kind of enough to read this early and offer a blurb or early review. Your kind words always make me gush.

And to my partner and our kids. This last year has been incredibly difficult and we are still struggling to get from one day to the next. I think this book probably reflects that in its consistent hopelessness and dread. Horror is a reflection of life and our fears. It seems that, as of late, I am full of them. And yet my family hasn't gotten rid me yet. Fingers crossed they never do!

About the Author

Wesley Winters is the author of several dozen stories, including those found in *Nobody's Savior, Terrible Lizards, WMP Dark Fiction Magazine,* and the second volumes of *Horror-Scope: A Zodiac Anthology* and *That Old House: The Bathroom.* He primarily writes dark fiction and queer fiction. He is a married father of three, and an autism advocate.

www.wintrymonsterspress.com
Instagram and Threads @WintryMonstersPress
Contact@wintrymonsterspress.com